Permanent

Ink

Deadwalkers

By
R.W.K. Clark

Published in the United States by Clarkltd.
Po Box 45313 Rio Rancho, NM 87174
info@clarkltd.com

Edition 1

United States Copyright Office
#TX 8-354-882 December 2016
Library of Congress Control Number: 2017907161
International Standard Book Numbers
ISBN-10: 0997876735
ISBN-13: 9780997876734
ASIN: B01N6QNUWL

/200801

CONTENTS

ACKNOWLEDGMENTS

I dedicate this novel to my wonderful readers and for all the amazing people I've met and those I haven't. To my family and loved ones, all your support will not be forgotten.

This book was made possible by reviews from readers like you.

Thank you

R.W.K. Clark

PROLOGUE

Dr. Randy Carstens sat quietly in his office at Aspen Stationers' Supply Company. He was the only person remaining in the laboratory area, for all the other employees, except for some of the bigwigs upstairs, had gone home to their families and hot meals. Randy was practically a slave among the Aspen ranks. It seemed the only hot meal he had enjoyed in months had the word 'InstaDinner' emblazoned on the front of the rectangular box.

His office was dark, except for the circle of light from his desk lamp, which illuminated the blotter and the scattering of paperwork which covered it. His forefingers were steepled under his chin, supporting a face which bore a very solemn expression. His brown, rheumy eyes stared at one solitary sheet of paper on his desk, but only for moments at a time. Randy would periodically close his lids, and a tear or two would ooze out from under them, battle his mediocre lashes, and trickle down his damp cheeks.

He opened his eyes yet again, this time even swiping briefly at his cheek before returning his hand and fingers to their original position beneath his chin. His eyes shifted to a framed photo on his desk next to his telephone—his wife and two young sons. A slight smile flickered at the corners of his mouth, then faded rapidly, only to be replaced with a grimace of pain. He clamped his eyes shut once again.

His mind shot to the memory of the meeting earlier that day. He had tried to reason and talk sense to the board members. He had even practically thrown his argument to the mercy of the two men he knew the most, Roger McGinley, the CEO, and Thaddeus Greer, the CFO. Greer was actually siding with him, that release of the new product needed to be postponed so more in-depth testing could be done. The man had buckled in the meeting, and ultimately ended up a slave to the political machine; Thaddeus Greer voted for timely release just like all the rest of them.

Randy allowed his eyelids to flicker open yet another time, and this time they settled back on the sheet of paper on his desk, the one on the top of the pile. The light from the lamp glistened off a bold scribble of senseless ink on the sheet, causing rainbow-like reflections of color to seemingly bounce around within its own bounds. The holographic effect of the ink was beautiful, almost hypnotizing. It was like no other ink the company made before.

Randy sat forward and took hold of the sheet, then sat back once again. He held the sheet before his face, blocking and shading the lamplight. The bold scribble and all of its three-dimensional hues continued their crazy dance on the white surface, even in the shadows.

They seemed to be even more pronounced in the darkness if that were at all possible. Randy shook his head in disgust and tossed the sheet back onto the desk.

He leaned forward once again and took hold of a pen with a hot pink plastic casing. The words 'Aspen Lumiosa' were scrawled on the grip in black cursive; it was followed by smaller words in simple Roman lettering: 'Wide Point.' Randy held it by the end in the light, between his forefinger and thumb, and rolled the tubular casing back and forth. Another tear pooled in his left eye and rolled down his cheek.

Without force or anger, he tossed the pen across the room. It hit the wall next to the office door and dropped to the tile floor with a light clatter. Randy sat back again and let his mind wander back to the meeting. He hadn't tried hard enough, he hadn't been nearly as forceful with his argument as he should have, but then again, he had never done anything with force or passion in his life, now, had he?

∞

"We are on the verge of bankruptcy, and the Lumiosa series is going to pull us out." Roger McGinley spoke with a toothy, flashing grin, turning on the charm for the rest of the board to see. "It really is very simple: we release the Lumiosa, right now, on the dawn of a new school year, and I can tell you that this particular item will save us from a sealed fate, people."

Randy had spoken up once again at that point. He had already presented the problems they were encountering with the Lumiosa in testing, but McGinley had continued to shift the focus to Aspen's doomed bottom line, and it seemed that no one cared about the truth. He felt powerless and frustrated.

"Mr. McGinley," he said. Then he paused and coughed nervously into his fist, his eyes shifting around the table, glancing quickly at each and every one of the board members. "You realize that, while beautiful and definitely attractive to consumers, some of the testing results are quite... disturbing. We need to do a bit of tweaking, or there is no telling what the consequences will be."

Greer spoke up. "You know, Randy, I am in agreement with your apprehensions." The man took a deep breath. "But you have admitted that once the ink dries any potential danger is immediately obliterated, and you also admit that it will be fine if the wet ink doesn't come into direct contact with broken skin. You and your boys pretty much soaked the lab subjects in Lumiosa, am I correct?"

"Yes, but..."

Greer crossed his arms over his chest and sat back in his chair. "I would guess, and it would only be a guess, that the chances of some type of similar adverse reaction in a human would be very slim." He went into brief thought, clicked his tongue, and continued. "I mean, even if the Lumiosa product were to come into contact, hypothetically speaking, with say, an open wound, the consumer would be getting a minute fraction, in the millionths, of what the subjects were exposed to. And it takes only what, twenty, thirty seconds to dry, maximum?"

"Yes, but…"

"Well, I think it's obvious that moving on with the release is the only way to go," McGinley interrupted. "If we don't, we will have to wrap up Aspen altogether, folks, and that is the hard cold truth." His eyes were steely and cold, not matching the broad smile on his face. They focused forcefully on Randy, making him feel shifty and jittery. "If the real numbers show it is going to be safe, well, that is what we are going to go by, Dr. Carstens."

Randy couldn't simply allow the meeting to wrap up and for the truth to be blown over so easily. "Mr. McGinley," he blurted with a wee bit of assertiveness to his tone, "I don't know how small a dose will affect anyone; we haven't had time to minimize exposure to find the proper range! I tell you—no, I implore you—" he looked around the table, actually making eye contact with each and every person there, "Do not release the Lumiosa! Now, I know that I can concentrate on the studies, get them done on a smaller, faster scale. And I will even promise to have any needed changes complete in, say, five, six months."

"Five or six months!" The smile disappeared from McGinley's face as he tossed a small stack of presentation paperwork down the length of the boardroom table. The sheets flew here and there, some of them coming close to another board member at the far end, Jill Schmidt. She flinched and jerked away from them, as if afraid of whatever was written on them.

"That simply is not acceptable, people! We have thirty days from today, and the doors will be shut!" He stood and paced back and forth behind his chair at the head of the table. Finally, he stopped and put both fists down on the tabletop and leaned forward, his face flushed and sweating. "It's as simple as this, folks. Dr. Carstens and his crew have been in contact with Lumiosa all day, every day, for eight months. He is fine! Each and every one of his team is fine. We are going to proceed with a vote…"

∞

Just remembering the meeting, the tension at the table, the vote, and the subsequent victory for McGinley regarding the release of the Lumiosa pen series made Randy want to throw up. He didn't care what kind of verbal square dance McGinley had done, the fact remained that Randy firmly believed—no, not believed—knew, that this was going to turn out badly. Very badly, indeed.

He rapidly shook his head back and forth as if trying to clear it, then he plucked a tissue from the box on his desk and blew his nose hard. Randy then took a deep breath and stood up. He crossed the room and plucked his suit coat off a wooden coat tree by the door, put it on, and left the office, locking it firmly behind him.

He was in no position to quit; it was more essential now than ever that he presses on in testing and make any alterations to the Lumiosa formula that were necessary. He would buck up, brush it off, and put his nose to the grindstone. Tonight, though, he would go home to his family and get a little rest.

He walked down the hallway, his shoes clicking on the hard floor of the corridor. The next door to the left read, 'Laboratory.' A long window followed that; it was covered on the inside by closed blinds. At certain points, he could see the dim lighting from inside the lab trying to escape through tiny holes.

Randy inserted his key and opened the door. With a flick of the light switch, the lab became bright like the day, and he could hear squealing and scurrying immediately. Time to do one final check on the subjects before he left. They had been exposed to a much smaller amount of Lumiosa in the far cage, and they were new rats. Any negative effects would show already if the ink stayed true to form, and Randy suspected that it would.

A loud, squeaky scream suddenly came from the far cages, making Randy nearly jump out of his skin. He pulled himself together in only seconds and made a dash for the area. He was about seven feet from the cage when he was stopped dead in his tracks by what he saw.

Randy continued to step forward, trembling, his lip shaking, and his eyes wide with fear. The sight was horrid, and it was just as bad as it had been for all the others. The smaller exposure hadn't mattered at all. He simply stood finally, frozen in his place, horrified.

CHAPTER 1

"I can get whatever supplies I want because I'm in middle school," Megan told her younger sister Melanie with mock contempt. "You're only in baby school."

Melanie bristled and slammed her spoon down on the surface of the kitchen table, causing her bowl of Cocoa Cosmos to bounce slightly. "I'm not a baby, and I'm not in baby school. You're a brat, and that's all! Mom!"

Michelle Casperson turned around abruptly from putting cereal boxes into the cupboard. "All right, all right! That's enough. Now, I want you both to finish your breakfast, without talking! If you want to go shopping for supplies today rather than this weekend, you are going to want to do as I say, girls. I won't hesitate to postpone our little trip; school doesn't start until Monday."

Both girls fell into immediate silence and began spooning cereal into their mouths. Michelle smiled at the fact that her bluffing worked. Today was actually the only day she had to take them for new school clothing and supplies; she would be busy volunteering for the church garage sale all weekend.

She stood and reveled in the silence and began flipping through a flier from Marceau's, a clothing store for kids. She had a stack of similar fliers beneath that one: two for shoes another for actual supplies. She had their shopping day planned to a tee, for it was one of the girls' favorite days of the year.

Michelle got to the flier for the supplies. The front page had smiling kids with backpacks on; the backpack prices were listed for two popular brands, and that was all. She turned to the first page, and the first thing she saw was exactly what she had been looking for: the pens. The Aspen Lumiosa series which Megan had been so excited about.

The pens were five dollars apiece. Michelle raised her eyebrows in surprise. Well, Megan will be getting only one of these today, she thought. She was sure Melanie would want one as well, even though she wasn't allowed pens in grade school, but Michelle could understand. She had seen a commercial for the pen, and she had to admit, she was tempted to pick one up for herself to play with.

According to the commercial, the new pens, by Aspen, had this crazy ink which was highly colorful, almost holographic in appearance. On the television ad, it was actually very beautiful. Michelle had to admit that she didn't see a scholastic purpose of any kind for the pen, except for maybe artwork. Aspen had brilliantly begun marketing for the product just a month ago, right before school was set to open—the pens were going on sale today. Yes, they were smart and sneaky indeed.

Suddenly, the two girls were behind her, plopping their bowls, spoons, and glasses hurriedly into the sink. Michelle jumped, startled, and turned to them. "Nope! Rinse and load, little ladies. Rinse and load."

Her daughters groaned but proceeded to do as they were told. Michelle snatched up the fliers and grabbed her purse from the kitchen table and put it over her shoulder. "I'm going to start the van. I'll see you out there in a bit. Megan, make sure to lock the garage door behind you; the rest of the house is already locked up."

Michelle went into the garage and started the van, then backed out and down the driveway, where she put it into park and leaned out to check the mailbox. After that, she looked back into the garage, at the door to the house. In only seconds her daughters emerged, and Melanie came running full-speed for the van while Megan locked the door and closed it.

Suddenly Melanie tripped, her toe catching on an uneven spot in the paved driveway. She fell forward hard, landing with an audible 'oooff!' facedown. Immediately the nine-year-old girl began to wail, and Michelle jumped from the van while Megan darted for her little sister, who continued crying loudly from her position on the ground.

They reached her at the same time, and Megan began to help her up. "I'm always tellin' ya to slow down, Mel! Why do you gotta run all the time?"

Michelle knelt before her younger child as she shot a glare at the older. "Are you okay? Are you hurt, Melly?"

Melanie's wailing subsided, and she began to sniffle

as she bent her arm at the elbow to show them the back of her forearm. The flesh there was scraped and torn, but it was only skin. The side of her hand, however, was torn a bit more, and it was bleeding, but only slightly.

"Oh, honey," Michelle soothed. "Let's go in and put some peroxide on it before we go."

"No!" Melanie quickly got to her feet and wiped at her eyes with the back of her hand. "I'm fine, Mommy! It stings, but it will go away fast. Let's go shopping."

Michelle slowly stood and looked her daughter up and down; the girl was already on her way to the running van at the end of the drive. The woman glanced at Megan, who shrugged, rolled her eyes, and joined her sister. "Ugh! These kids are going to be the death of me," she said under her breath, and then she also made her way back to the van.

All of the stores she had chosen for shopping were close to their suburban home in Thornton, Colorado. Michelle hated not only the Denver freeway traffic, but she also hated the extensiveness of using it; it could take an hour just to get across town, and she simply didn't have the patience. She determined years ago that any shopping ever would be done close to home, short of a special need. So, the trio set out for the short drive to Marceau's; they would get clothes first.

Michelle put the radio on a pop station, and all three of them sang along to the latest hit by some bubblegum blonde whose name seemed to evade her for the time being. She glanced into her review mirror and watched her daughters bopping and singing with all their might.

The scraped arm was forgotten, and Michelle gave a sigh of relief through her smile.

Soon she pulled the van into the lot at the Mountain View Mall and glanced at the clock on her dash: nine thirteen. Cars were already parked, but the place wasn't too packed, which was exactly what Michelle had been hoping for. She glanced around as she drove around the massive building, still humming to the radio and a song by a boy group she recognized as being called the Three Lads. As she neared Marceau's, she took note that there were many more cars there than she had anticipated, and she wound up taking a parking spot about ten slots from the entrance to the store.

"Alrighty, girlies! Let's hit it!" She put the van in park and turned off the ignition. She quickly turned to the two girls in the backseat, who were removing their seatbelts with trembling excitement. "Ground rules: four regular outfits apiece plus two sets of gym clothes. That's all you get in here, bottom line. Don't even try begging for more, or we will leave pronto, got it?"

"Got it," they both replied in unison.

In minutes they were in Marceau's. The place had about three small families besides the Casperson's, so Michelle was extremely relieved that they had gotten such an early start. It would make the day go smoothly, and it would make the task fun.

It took them nearly an hour and a half to get the sets of clothes she had budgeted for, and it turned out to be a blast. The experience was filled with laughter, teasing, and a lot of catwalk posing accompanied by dramatic gestures and expressions. Michelle made sure to get plenty of photos on her cell, and wound up posting some to her favorite social media account. The girls were beautiful, and they both glowed with their excitement.

Next, the trio tooled in the van to the shoe store, where they purchased two pairs of the latest and greatest sneakers and two more pairs of dressier shoes. Only one time was there any grief, and it came from Melanie, who had decided that she was more than ready for lunch. Michelle decided that the next stop would be the Burger Blast restaurant, which was halfway between the shoe store and Thornton Community Rexall, which was where they would get the supplies. The drugstore happened to have much, much more than prescription and non-prescription medication. It was a go-to merchant as far as stationery and office supplies as well.

Lunch was a relaxing indulgence of burgers, fries, and pop, followed by Melanie playing on the indoor toys which the restaurant provided. Michelle watched her daughter through a glass wall, and then glanced at Megan. The girl was watching her sister as well, but she had a look of longing on her face. She had refused to play at first, claiming she was too 'old' for baby games.

"You know," Michelle began slowly, "you are never too old, especially if your body is still the right size to enjoy the toys, Meg."

The girl turned to her mother, then began to look almost frantically around the dining area. Michelle smiled as she observed this, and her smile grew when

Megan appeared satisfied that no one she knew was there. She jumped up and ran through the door to have a little fun.

So, their tightly planned outing ended up running just a little late. Michelle simply couldn't cut off the girls when they were actually playing together, so happy and carefree. She watched as they ran from toy to toy together, Megan's arm protectively flung over her little sister's shoulders. It was the best they had gotten along in quite some time, and their mother wouldn't ruin it. She finally made a short video to post later on, mentally shaking her head at her own behavior.

Thirty minutes later they pulled into Community Rexall and parked as close to the door as they could. Michelle took note that the girls were starting to poop out, and she certainly craved a second wind herself. She thought she would stop at CoffeeUp for a cappuccino when they were finished shopping, and she would get a smoothie for the girls as well.

"Okay," she began as the girls unbuckled for the fourth time. "We're almost done. How are my troops feeling?"

Megan glanced at her. "Good mom. Let's get this done now, all right?"

She smiled at her daughter. "Got it. Now, only one of these…" She paused to glance at the ad, which was open on the seat next to her. "…Lumiosa pens for each of you. They are pretty pricey, so only one."

Both girls sluggishly nodded, and they all hopped out of the minivan and headed for the store. Inside, they quickly found the school supply aisle, and Michelle looked at it with shock. It was pretty torn up, with notebooks and folders scattered about, and gaping holes where things had been hanging but had been purchased.

"Wow, I'm glad we got here when we did," she said with a shake of her head. She fished two folded sheets of paper from her oversized bag: school supply lists.

"Megan first," she began. "A binder, seven folders, and some loose-leaf paper." Megan found the items and put them in the cart after choosing what she wanted. "Also, both of you should choose your backpacks now." The girls obeyed.

Michelle nodded, pleased. "Okay, your dad got your laptop last week, so we can skip that. Pencils, sharpener, erasers, and pens are next. Listen, get a pack of regular pens, besides the Lumiosa, okay? You can't do assignments with that thing."

Megan quickly gathered the first items, as well as a package of black gel pens. She dumped them quickly into the cart, then went to the end of the aisle and stood before the Aspen Lumiosa display. The pens consisted of a variety of colored casings, with black cursive lettering on the front.

"Get whatever color you want, but they all write with the same ink, remember?" Michelle asked.

The girl took only seconds to choose a pen with a purple casing. She turned to her mother, her face glowing. "I just can't wait to get home and use this!" She skipped to the cart and put it in.

"I'm going to get mine now, Mom," Melanie said,

and Michelle nodded at her. She ran up and snatched a pink version, stopping only to read the cardboard packaging. "Broad point. That's what I want!"

Melanie's list was more basic: glue, tissues, scissors, pencils, and the like. She also needed construction paper, so they had to visit the arts and crafts aisle, as there was none with the school supplies. Soon, the three of them were checking out and packing the van with their purchases to head home.

Michelle made a stop for coffee and smoothies, and before they knew it, they were pulling into the driveway at home. As they took their purchases inside Michelle smiled to herself; it had not only gone fast, it had been fun, and the girls had behaved wonderfully. She would let them play with their pens after supper if they wanted. Might as well enjoy them at five bucks a pop.

She was secure in the thought that her family would have a wonderful Friday evening.

R.W.K. Clark

CHAPTER 2

Brian Olson sat in his room, his laptop open and alight, his concentration focused on a rap video he had been dying to see which had come out that very day. It was Friday afternoon, and his mother, Kathy, would be home from work at any moment. She told him that morning that she would pick up a few things from his school supply list on her way home, so he expected her to be a bit late. When she was home she forbade him to hang on the computer, so he wanted to get it in while he had a chance.

Brian was going to be in the ninth grade, and he was pretty excited about it; Monte Vista high school, at last! Sure, he was nervous about actually attending the high school itself because he would be going from being a big fish in a small pond to the complete opposite, but he also knew all of the kids in his class, and he was pretty confident in himself to boot. There would be no problems there. After all, he had been born in Monte Vista, and he had lived there his entire life; he knew almost all the other kids.

He found himself quickly growing bored with the game he was playing on the computer, so he checked his Faceplace newsfeed; as usual, nothing had changed there, so he put his old desktop computer to sleep and sat back in his chair. Glancing at the clock told him that a snack would be a good idea, so finally, he rose and went to the kitchen, where he put some pizza rolls in the microwave.

While they were cooking, the telephone rang. Brian jumped, startled, then picked up the cordless receiver from its base. It was likely his mother, calling to make sure he had cleaned his room so she wouldn't have to look at his mess when she got home; he had.

"Hello?"

"Hey, Brian. It's Caleb," the voice replied. "What's up?"

Brian smiled a bit. Caleb had been his best friend since second grade; his calls were always welcome. He was a bit surprised, though. His friend was supposed to have had plans that evening.

"Not much, man," Brian replied. "I thought your grandparents were having your family over for dinner."

Caleb clucked. "Yeah, they did, and then my grandmother took me for shoes, so the night wasn't as bad as I thought."

"What kind did you get?" Brian asked.

Caleb answered, "Those badass black and red Jdens. Can you believe it?"

"Lucky," Brian said in a sad voice. "My mom could never afford those things. I ended up getting a crappy pair of Fills 'cause they were on sale."

Caleb clucked his tongue yet again. "It's no biggie,

man. Fills aren't so bad, ya know? Heck, they used to be the stuff!"

"Yeah, but not now."

Caleb continued. "Anyway, I was calling because we ended up stopping off at OfficePeak so my granny could get some photo paper for her printer, ya know? While we were there, I showed her those Lumiosa pens. Since Mom wouldn't get one for me I turned on the charm, and my granny got me not one, but two! Can you believe it?"

Brian shook his head; fun stuff always happened to Caleb. He, too, had wanted one of those crazy pens, but they were pretty expensive. There was no way his mother could afford to get him even one, so he had asked once, gotten a 'no,' and dropped the subject. After all, they just came out for sale today, so he could always save up. These facts didn't stop him from feigning excitement for his best pal, though.

"Hey, that's cool, man," he replied. "You're a lucky dog."

Caleb was still for a moment. "Well, you know the only reason I asked for two was so you could have one too, dontcha?"

"Really, bro?"

His friend chuckled. "Really. Anyway, I'm home, so if it's okay with your mom, I thought I would run it over real quick."

Caleb Reardon only lived down the block, and the sun was just going down, so Brian excitedly agreed. He had wanted one of those Lumiosas ever since the commercials came out a few weeks before. He did a lot of art, and it would be one of the coolest colors in his collection of pens and pencils. He hung up and turned the pizza rolls, put them back in, and went to the front window to wait for his pal.

Within a minute he saw him coming up the sidewalk; he must have jogged! Brian grabbed the key to the double deadbolt his mom had put on the front and used it to open the door and let him into the living room, where they immediately knocked knuckles. Caleb was wearing a new Colorado Rockies cap that Brian loved.

"Awesome hat, man," he said. "You want some pizza rolls?"

Caleb grinned. "You know it! I gotta be home in a half-hour. Are they cooking?"

Just then the microwave alarm rang. "They're done," Brian said. "Got some soda, too, if you want one."

Out in the kitchen, Brian fished two cans of soda out of the fridge and then got the plate of snacks from the microwave. When he turned to set the items on the counter, Caleb was holding out a flat package made of cardboard and plastic. A neon green pen was nestled inside; green was his favorite color.

"Here ya go, bro," he said. "I'd never forget about you; I've got your back!"

Brian smiled and put down the plate and two pops. He took the package and looked at it, his eyes lighting up. It sure looked kind of plain for what it could do, at least on the commercial.

"Have you tried it out yet? Yours, I mean," he asked Caleb.

Caleb nodded. "Yeah, and it's super freakin' cool. I'm tellin' ya." He grabbed a hot pizza roll and began to toss it back and forth in his hands like a solo game of hot potato.

Just then the side door to the house opened, and Kathy Olson walked in, her purse over her shoulder and her hands full of plastic shopping bags. Dark circles of exhaustion were under her eyes, but as soon as she saw the boys, her eyes lit up.

"Hey, kiddos!" she exclaimed. "What's happening?"

Caleb stopped tossing his snack. "Hi, Mrs. Olson. Just hanging out for a bit. I gotta be home in a little bit, though."

Brian put his pen down on the countertop. "Hey, Mom. Just having something to eat. Is there more stuff in the car?"

Kathy set the sacks down on the kitchen table and followed them with her purse. "No," she replied as she plopped down in a chair to remove her sensible heels from her aching feet. "I managed to get it all. These are the rest of the supplies on your list, Bri, so you should be good."

Shoes off, she stood and walked up to the boys. Caleb was chewing on a pizza roll, another in hand, and Brian was taking a drink from his soda. Kathy hugged him from behind and kissed him on the neck before tousling his hair.

"You are getting so big; you're taller than me!" she

said. "Soon you'll tower above Uncle Jim."

Noticing the pen on the counter, Kathy picked it up and looked it over. "Is this that fancy ink pen you wanted?"

Brian nodded. "Yeah," he replied slowly. "Um, Caleb's grandma picked them up, and he brought one for me."

Kathy's eyes shifted to the other boy. "These things are five dollars apiece, Caleb," she said. "Does your grandmother know you brought one to Brian?"

The young man swallowed his mouthful of food nearly whole. "Yes, ma'am. I told her the second one was for Brian."

Kathy looked down at the pen again. "How embarrassing."

"Mrs. Olson," Caleb quickly said, "it's no big deal. You know my mom loves you. My granny doesn't mind at all. They love Brian too; he's like my brother or something."

Kathy's shot a glare at her son. "Did you ask them to do this?"

"No Mom!" he replied. "Caleb just surprised me with it! I promise."

"I surprised him with it, Mrs. Olson, I swear!" Caleb had another pizza roll, but it was frozen in mid-air, about eight inches from his mouth, as he waited to see how the uncomfortable situation played out.

Kathy turned the cardboard package over, reading the back silently. After a moment she read aloud, "Warning: Do not touch ink when wet. Highly smearable. For best results allow to dry completely before coming into contact with skin or clothing." She paused, then said, "Why is that written as a 'warning,' do you think?"

Caleb shrugged, and Brian replied, "Probably just because it smears really bad; that would ruin someone's art. I'm glad you read that, Mom. I would have been mad if I ruined my stuff by smearing it."

"Don't you read the instructions, Bri?" she asked.

Her son looked at her as if she were plumb crazy. "On an ink pen, Mother?"

Kathy chuckled. "I guess not. That does sound crazy."

The three of them laughed, and then Caleb polished off his pop and said, "I better go. My mom will have my head if I'm even ten seconds late." He gave Brian a firm clasp on the shoulder. "See ya tomorrow, eh, mano?"

"Yep," Brian replied. "See ya. Have a good night."

With Caleb gone, Kathy turned to her son. "I believe Caleb surprised you, Brian, so I'm not going to gripe too much. But next time, simply say thanks and refuse. It's terribly embarrassing for me as a single parent to not be able to afford things for you, and we are not a charity case. Not for the Reardon's or anyone else."

Brian nodded. "Got it, Mom. Do you want me to do anything for you before I go to my room? I'm gonna play with my pen a bit."

"No," she replied. "Just take your supplies and load your backpack up for Monday, okay?"

He gave her a firm hug. "Okay. I love ya, you know?"

"I know, and I love you, too."

Back in his room, Brian did as he was told and loaded up his old backpack. When he was finished, he pulled a couple of sheets of blank paper out of his ancient printer.

"Ouch! Damn it!" Brian cried.

The fresh papercut began to bleed as he inserted his finger to his mouth. Brian sat down and opened the packaging of his pen, to see what it was capable of. He was excited to see if the ink really looked like it did on television.

He uncapped it and began writing his first and last name scrawled in large letters on the paper. Brian then stopped and looked at his work. Sure enough, the ink was bright and filled with strong, reflective color which was so three-dimensional one would think they could fall into it. He smiled, thrilled. Next, in order to test the 'smear-ability,' he ran his fingers over it. The ink smeared so badly it seemed to follow his fingers across the page.

Brian held up his hand and looked at his fingers. The ink was bold on his skin, and the coverage was so good, even second-hand, that it completely covered the papercut he had on his forefinger. He raised his eyebrows with surprise.

"Okay, pen people, I guess you meant it when you said it would smear," he mumbled quietly. He crumpled the paper with his name and tossed it into the wastebasket next to his desk.

Brian decided he would do his name in graffiti letters and tape it down on the cover of his binder. It would be really cool, and more than likely Caleb would want him to make one for him. He put the pen to the clean sheet and got to work.

This had to be the coolest pen Brian had ever seen.

R.W.K. Clark

CHAPTER 3

Randy sat stationary on a spinning stool in his lab. His eyes were fixed on his rats, and his stomach was lurching with nausea and disgust.

Before him, up and down the length of the laboratory countertop, were seven large cages, each with three rats in them. Each represented the last seven days of testing, and not one of the subjects looked good. To put it mildly, Randy was completely mortified.

He had continued to reduce the amount of ink he was exposing the rats too, and not only that, he was exposing less and less of their flesh to the ink as well. At first, he had thought that the ink had negative effects only if it got through broken skin, due to the first one having a small cut on one of its feet. Unfortunately, in the last week, he had learned that the ink itself would cause a severe rash, which resulted in broken skin as well. In other words, the ink was 'helping itself.'

The animals in the cages were horrendous. They continually attacked each other, eating and gnawing.

There was no stopping this, no reversing of it. He had tried everything he could think of to kill them, even going so far as to put on his metal chain gloves and stab at a pair of the rodents over and over. His only solution was to pour acid on them to dispose of them.

Randy was at a loss, and he had no idea what to do or how to proceed.

He was due in yet another meeting in fifteen minutes, this time to update the board on the 'progress' he had made in rectifying the issue. There was no progress, nor did he believe there ever would be. Next to him, on the counter opposite the rats, sat his folder. In it was all the information, including photos, regarding his findings. He was going to demand that they take the pens off the shelves immediately.

If they refused, he would go directly to the authorities and turn the folder over to them.

A knock came on the door behind him. Randy spun around, and through the window on the door he could see Roger McGinley, his fake smile almost glowing through the glass. Randy smirked at the man and rose to let him in. He reached the door quickly and opened it.

"I'll be up directly," he said to the CEO. "I'm prepared to present my findings."

McGinley stepped into the lab and Randy let the door close. He walked back to his stool, his back to the man, who was closing the shade that covered the window on the door. As he did so, he saw the rats for the first time.

"Wow, Carstens," he said in a low voice.

Randy turned to the man, whom he now hated. McGinley's face was void of any smile now. He was pale, and he looked as if he may throw up.

"This is what it does," he said matter-of-factly. "This ink of yours."

McGinley approached the cages and stood, frozen, before them. He watched in horror as the rats continued to go at each other. A couple of them were even in the stage of coming back to life. It was terrible and unnatural, it was downright evil!

"You have been telling me about this, but…"

"But what, sir?" Randy asked in a sarcastic voice. "But you thought I was making it up? But you thought it was a joke? But what?"

McGinley continued staring. "I guess I thought you were exaggerating. What do you really think are the chances of this product having the same effect on human beings? Percentage-wise, I mean."

"One hundred percent," Randy replied in a quiet voice.

That got Roger McGinley's attention, and he abruptly turned to the scientist. "Well, Lumiosa has been on the market since yesterday; there is no way to get them off the shelves. They have been selling like crazy, and the projections are outstanding."

"You have to recall them, sir," Randy said. "Immediately."

McGinley shook his head. "No. I'm not going to do that."

Randy felt rage build in his entire body. He stood up and approached his boss, reaching him in two long strides. "You have to. I guarantee you that people, children especially, are going to die! Are you out of your mind?"

The CEO suddenly laughed. "Don't be naïve, Carstens. The numbers are so good that we are going to be out of trouble within the month. There have been no reports of any issues whatsoever. No, I won't do it."

"It takes only a few hours for the effects to manifest, McGinley!" Randy was so angry he was shaking. He took a series of deep breaths, and when he was a bit calmer, he stated in a clear controlled voice, "If you don't do this, I am going to the authorities with my findings. It's as simple as that."

Now McGinley spun around to face Randy, his face red with anger. "Don't you try to threaten me. I'll see to it that you not only lose your job but that no one ever hears your lame opinions." The man was clenching and unclenching his fists rapidly. "As a matter of fact, you don't need to attend the meeting at all. I will present your findings; you clean out your office and get the heck out of the building within the half-hour."

Randy's mouth hung open as he stared at the man in disbelief. How could one human being be so greedy and so calloused as the man before him seemed to be? His eyes glanced to the left at the file folder on the counter, and McGinley took note of it immediately. He walked over and picked up the folder marked 'Lumiosa Trials.'

"Well, this was all I need to seal the deal anyway, thank you," McGinley said. "A half-hour and I mean it. The meeting will take ten minutes or less; I'll be back to make sure you are gone."

With that, the man left the lab, leaving Randy to

decide what to do. Without the folder, there wasn't much he could do. He had the same information in his computer though, so he decided to go there right away, send the computer files to his personal cloud service, and then go to the police as quickly as possible.

There was no other way.

∞

Roger McGinley sped to the elevator and got to the top floor boardroom as quickly as he could. He had the folder in his hands, which would make the series of lies he was about to tell look very good indeed. If the board wanted copies, well, he would simply forge some convincing and dishonest copies for their benefit.

He saw absolutely no reason to take the Lumiosa series off the shelves. He knew if he did it would mean sure death for Aspen Stationers' Supply, and he wasn't going to let that happen. He had worked here since he was twenty, and he had worked his way up the ladder with all of his heart. If Aspen fell apart because of a little fluke with their most popular ink, it wouldn't be on his watch.

The CEO got to the boardroom and, flashing his dazzling smile, excitedly told the board about Carstens' *success* rectifying the pens' issues. He waved the file folder around convincingly, and he let the members know that Carstens had to go home to deal with an ill child. Everyone left the eight-minute-long powwow happy and satisfied, with plenty of laughter and slapped backs.

After McGinley had taken the folder to his office

and locked it safely in his desk, he headed back to Carstens' office and lab. He wanted to make sure the guy was out, and he was going to stay with him until he was. It wouldn't do to have the guy blabbing to anyone with the truth of the matter, and he would see to it that he didn't.

So, he took the elevator down to confront the scientist once again, humming brightly during the entire ride.

CHAPTER 4

"Mom, something is wrong with Melanie. I think she's sick or something."

It was twelve forty-two in the morning, and Michelle had just finally fallen asleep. She was exhausted, but that fact hadn't brought her to sleep any easier; it was always difficult for her to rest soundly when her husband, Mitch, was out of town. It was late Friday night now, and he wouldn't be home from Chicago until Monday evening.

Her eyes fluttered open, and she groaned as she strained in the darkness at the person standing next to her bed. By height, she could tell it was Megan. What was she doing up so late, and what had she just said?

"Megan?" she asked in a groggy voice. "What's going on? Why are you up?"

The girl reached out in the darkness and turned on her mother's bedside lamp, causing Michelle's hand to fly up to her face to protect her eyes from its glare.

"Melanie's sick, Mom," she answered. "You need to get up."

Michelle nodded and swung her feet to the floor and put them into her pink fuzzy slippers. "What's wrong with her?"

Megan shrugged and rubbed at her own eyes with her fists. "I don't know. I was sleeping, and I heard her crying or something, so I got up to find out what was wrong. She's all sweaty and red, and she's breathing really hard." The girl turned to leave the room, then stopped and turned around. "Oh, and she was, like, crying in her sleep. She never even woke up when I went in, and I tried to wake her up three times."

Michelle stood and followed her older child out of the room and down the hall to Melanie's room. The door was ajar, and the girl's nightlight was casting a yellow hue and throwing shadows. She approached the girl's bed and turned her princess lamp on.

"Melly?" she said. "It's Mommy, honey. Wake up."

The girl didn't move or open her eyes. She groaned and whimpered for a moment, then went still again. Michelle brushed her daughter's sweat-soaked hair off her forehead, and immediately her hand jerked back. Her eyes widened, and she turned abruptly to Megan.

"Get me the ear thermometer out of the hall closet, bug," she said, then turned back to Melanie as Megan jogged out of the room. "Melly, I need you to wake up."

Michelle began to gently shake the girl, but all that did was cause the whimpering to start up again. She noticed that the blankets had been kicked completely off, and she reached for them to pull them back up; they were completely soaked! Her stomach flip-flopped with concern.

Megan returned. "Her you go, Mom. Is she okay?"

"I don't know," Michelle replied as she removed the cap from the earpiece and put it in her daughter's ear. "Let's just get a temp first."

Within seconds the gadget beeped, and Melanie's temperature appeared on the small screen: 103.7.

"Megan, get me a clean blanket out of the linen closet, then put some shoes on and go start the car and open the garage," she said. "We're going to the emergency room. Go now!"

The girl disappeared again, and within only seconds she returned toting a single-sized quilt. She handed it to her mother without saying a word and then left yet again to obey the directives she had been given. Michelle stood and unfolded the blanket with a couple of shakes, then wrapped it around her daughter's sweaty body.

"We're going to the doctor, Melly," she said soothingly. "They're just going to check you and make sure that you are okay."

She heaved the girl up and let her head rest on her shoulder, then she covered her head with the corner of the quilt. Walking as quickly as she could she made her way downstairs, where she slipped her feet into a pair of thongs which sat on a mat next to the garage door before leaving and clumsily shutting the door behind her.

Megan was in the passenger seat of the van, her seatbelt buckled. She had the vehicle running, and the garage door was open, just as Michelle had asked. Melanie was quickly put in the back seat, and then her mother jumped into the driver's seat and put the van in reverse. Her heart was pounding, and her mind was racing.

"Who have you two been around lately that is sick?" she asked Megan as she got moving down the road.

Megan tried to think about the question, but not a single ill person came to mind. "No one, Mom. We haven't even left the house since we went shopping with you. No, wait, Melly did play in the treehouse this morning, but she was alone, remember?"

Michelle nodded and picked up her speed. "I wonder what it is… maybe she ate something bad?"

"We've all eaten the same food, Mother," Megan replied.

They made the rest of the twenty-minute drive to the hospital in silence. When they finally pulled into Suburban Medical Center in Thornton Michelle drove directly to the entrance and threw the van into park. She got out and began to get Melanie out of the back as Megan turned the engine off and got out of the van, keys in her hand. Once the sick girl was in her mother's arms, the woman began to run into the emergency room as fast as she could.

The ER was teeming with people. Some were seated in chairs, and others were in wheelchairs. Some were pacing around anxiously while others slept with their heads on the shoulders of loved ones. Down a long hallway, someone was screaming in either grief or horrible pain.

Michelle took note of none of it, however. She made

a beeline for a nurse who was seated behind a large countertop desk area. The woman was on a computer, and she seemed unfazed by the chaos surrounding her.

"Excuse me," Michelle began. "My daughter is really, really sick. I need to see someone right away please."

The woman turned to her and pulled a large card from a rack next to the computer. "The girl's name?"

"Melanie Casperson," Michelle replied.

"Age?"

"She's nine," Michelle said. "Look, can't we do this from a room?"

The woman looked up and smiled robotically. "I'm sorry. We have to admit her through triage. What are her symptoms?"

Michelle sighed with exasperation. "Her sister woke me up and said she was sick. When I went to check on her, she had a fever of 103.7, and she was covered in sweat. She was crying a bit in her sleep, and she wouldn't wake up."

The nurse wrote furiously. "Go ahead and have a seat right over there." She stopped and gestured toward a row of orange chairs which were lined up in the corridor along a wall. Next to them was a large door marked 'Triage.' "One of the triage nurses will be with you momentarily."

"Thank you." Michelle turned to Megan and then nodded toward the chairs with her head. They walked over and sat down, Michelle cradling and rocking her sick younger child.

"Mom, just so you know, the van isn't parked, remember?"

Michelle thought about it only for a moment. "It's just going to have to stay there until we get her in a room. I can't leave her now."

At that exact moment, a young man of approximately twenty-seven came through the automatic doors leading outside. He wore a jacket with a nametag at the breast; both items identified him as a paramedic. He walked up to the main desk and said something to the nurse, which neither Michelle nor Megan could hear, and soon the nurse picked up the telephone receiver. She punched in a few numbers, and then her voice came over the PA system.

"Would the owners of the maroon minivan please move your vehicle," she firmly stated. "If not, the vehicle will be towed. Thank you."

The paramedic turned around and began to scan the room, and Michelle tried to stand quickly. He noticed and made his way toward her. As he walked, he held his hand up to signal her not to stand.

"Is that your van outside?" he asked.

Michelle nodded. Tears were forming in her eyes, and she felt completely overwhelmed. She felt Megan's hand on her shoulder, patting it and trying to console her.

"Yes," she replied. "My daughter is very sick. I'm waiting for the triage nurse to call us back. I can't leave."

Megan spoke up. "Mom, leave Melly with me; I'll sit

with her. It will only take you a minute."

The paramedic said, "I can stay here with the girls as well, but we really need your van to be moved right away. It's blocking the ambulance access."

Michelle looked over at Megan, studying her as if to be sure that the girl was alert enough to look after her sister. After a second she gave a single nod, and she put Melanie's limp, blanketed body into Megan's arms. Her brow was knit with anxiety.

"I'll be right back," she said, looking her oldest daughter dead in the eyes. "You stay right here no matter what, unless the nurse calls us, okay?"

Megan nodded. "I've got it, Mom."

With that, Michelle made her way out the automatic door. No sooner was she gone than the triage door opened, and a nurse with a clipboard appeared. She scanned the board for only a fraction of a second, then looked at Megan.

"Melanie Casperson?"

Megan sat up straight. "That's my sister, right here. She won't wake up."

The nurse looked around. "Do you have a parent with you?"

"Yes," the girl replied. "She had to move our car. She'll be right back."

The nurse began looking around yet again. "I need to get a wheelchair to bring her back in, okay, honey? Stay right here."

Megan watched the woman as she went a short distance up the corridor and took a right. In seconds she reappeared, pushing a wheelchair, her clipboard tucked snugly under her arm. She rushed toward the girls with the chair.

"Okay, hon," she began. "Just sit still, and I'll take your sister from you, okay?" She bent down and positioned her arms under Melanie properly. "At the count of three, I'm going to lift her, okay?"

Megan nodded, and the nurse said, "One, two, and three!" She lifted the girl almost effortlessly. Just as she was placing her in the chair, Michelle came through the door.

"Oh, thank you!" She hurried to them. "My daughter, she is so sick!"

The nurse smiled comfortingly at Michelle, but it had little effect on the woman. "Well, follow me Mrs...."

"Casperson," Michelle finished.

"Mrs. Casperson. We are going to find out what's going on with your daughter." She began to head back to the triage room pushing the chair. Megan and Michelle followed right on her heels.

When they were all the way into the room, the woman said, "I'm Julie Yates, and I'm the triage nurse this evening. I'm going to take Melanie's vitals. What's going on with her tonight?"

For the second time, Michelle recapped what she knew while the nurse took the child's temperature, pulse, and other vital signs. She also made it a point to try to wake Melanie, and when she was unsuccessful, she looked at her pupils with a light.

"I'm going to have to admit your daughter, Mrs. Casperson," she said as soon as she took the light from the girl's eyes. "A doctor should see her right away."

"What's wrong with her?" Michelle asked, her voice on the verge of panic.

The nurse held up her hand. "Just give me one moment." She left the room but returned less than a minute later. "We're going to take Melanie to a room. The nurse outside is getting a doctor here right now that can see her immediately. Her temperature is 104.6, and she is unresponsive. I am not able to make a diagnosis, ma'am. She needs to see a physician right away." She took hold of the wheelchair and began to steer it out of the room. "Follow me, please."

Ten minutes later they were in a room in the emergency department, with Melanie's still body tucked snugly under blankets on an exam table. Nurse Yates reassured them that the doctor would be there right away and that if anything should happen, they needed only to press the button on the end of a wire which was plugged into the wall and clipped to the bedding. Michelle took the chair next to the bed, and she sat rigidly, stroking her daughter's soaked hair.

Megan, on the other hand, paced back and forth as her mother cooed over her sister. Finally, she stopped. She stared at them both briefly.

"Mom," she said, "what's going on with Mel?"

Michelle answered her daughter without looking at her. "I think she just has a really bad flu bug."

"But why isn't she waking up?" Megan asked. "And

look, her skin is so... gray-looking."

Michelle only nodded at her daughter, exasperated and scared to death. At that moment a physician entered the room, accompanied by the nurse from the triage room. He offered Michelle a slight smile, attempting to put her at ease, but even she, in her panicked state, did not miss the stunned look on his face when he glanced at Melanie.

"I'm Dr. Kyle Hilliard," he said to Michelle as he walked directly to the sick child. He immediately lifted her eyelids and then proceeded to put his stethoscope in his ears. He turned to Julie Yates. "I want to start an IV immediately; she's terribly dehydrated. I also want the lab up here to draw for a CBC, stat."

The nurse ran out of the room, and Dr. Hilliard resumed his examination. He finished listening to her chest and began to take her pulse. "When did all this start?" he asked.

For what felt like the hundredth time, Michelle recounted all she knew to the doctor as he continued to examine the patient. While she spoke, Nurse Yates returned with two co-workers, and together they set about administering an IV for Melanie. Dr. Hilliard took the opportunity to speak with her quietly at that point, concern filling his dark eyes.

"What has she eaten?" he asked, and Michelle told him.

"Are any of her friends ill?" The answer was no.

He asked the same questions of Megan, who repeated the same. At last, he took a deep breath. He was obviously contemplative.

"Well, I have ordered complete blood work," he began. "I am going to also order IV antibiotics; is she allergic to anything?" Michelle shook her head, and he continued. "Well, I'm afraid I can't tell you much until her blood work comes back, except that you have a very sick girl. We are going to move her up to ICU, so if you need to go home and take care of anything, say, put on regular clothing, now would be the time, okay?"

"What if she wakes up and I'm gone?" she asked.

Dr. Hilliard put a comforting hand on her shoulder. "She'll be fine, but chances are she will take a bit. I'd go now if I were you. Oh, and who is your family doctor or pediatrician?"

"Moss," she replied. "Dr. Diana Moss."

"Fine," he said. "Nurse Yates, these two are going to run home real fast. Please get Melanie up to ICU as soon as possible before their return."

The woman nodded and went back to work. Michelle approached her youngest, who was surrounded by medical staff. Tears filled her eyes as she kissed her palm and touched the girl's leg with it.

"I'll be right back," she said. "I promise."

∞

Within the hour Michelle and Megan were back at home. Both showered, changed, and grabbed a quick bite to eat. Michelle called Mitch in Chicago and told him what was going on, and he told her he would catch the next flight back home that he could get on, which made her feel much better. Finally, both of them grabbed their cell phones and a tablet to keep Megan busy, and they left for the hospital once again.

"I just wish I had some idea where she could have contracted this craziness," Michelle mumbled as she drove.

Megan stared out the window into the early morning darkness. "Me too," she said. "One minute we were at the table, writing and drawing with our new pens. I remembered that she got tired fast, it seemed, but other than that she seemed fine. She just said she wanted to go to bed."

"She didn't say anything else? Nothing about feeling sick?"

Megan shook her head. "No. Just that she was done, and wanted to go to bed."

They fell into silence for the rest of the drive. Michelle shot a couple of prayers toward heaven, and Megan turned on her tablet and started playing a game. It was going to be a long night, and both of them knew it.

CHAPTER 5

Brian Olson lay in the darkness of his room watching the shadows being cast by the moonlight coming through his window. The box fan his mother bought for him five years ago blew cool air at his face, and normally it helped him sleep soundly. Tonight, however, it was lacking in its effectiveness. It was nearly one in the morning, and he hadn't slept a wink.

His stomach felt a bit queasy, and his joints were achy and sore. Brian was also sweating like a madman, and the fan did nothing whatsoever to relieve it. But it was the burning finger that was distracting him so.

The finger with the papercut that was the one. He had tested the wet holographic ink with it, and it had burned like crazy ever since. As a matter of fact, he looked at it right before bed, and it had turned a weird, pussy-looking gray-green. Brian had put triple antibiotic ointment on it and laid down, but the finger with the papercut was driving him mad.

He sat up on his elbow and grabbed the bottle of tropical flavored sports drink that he brought with him to bed. Breaking the cap, he put it to his lips and tilted his head back; even to his own surprise, he drained the twenty-four-ounce bottle of fluid in a single drink. Brian squinted at it in the darkness, tried to get one more sip, and then threw the bottle on the floor in frustration.

He could feel the heat coming from his eyes, and his head began to spin, so he lay back down on his pillow hard. Suddenly his bowels felt very loose and hot, and he thought he might heave right there in the bed. Leaning over toward his desk, Brian grabbed his wastepaper basket and leaned over it. He dry heaved many times before finally stopping to catch his breath. He was afraid he was going to crap his pants, but he didn't want to wake his mother; she would take him to the hospital or something.

Embarrassed, even in the privacy of his room, Brian flipped on his bedside lamp and swung his feet around to the floor. He glanced at the window and made sure there were no gaps in the blinds before he dropped his pajama pants and sat down on the garbage can as best he could.

The sound which came from the boy's bowels when he let go was horrid and unearthly, a guttural growl that reeked of death. Brian gagged and clasped his hand over his mouth as he filled the can with feces. It was nearly all water, but it smelled like the local water treatment plant, and once again he wanted to be sick.

It took him twenty minutes to finally be finished, and even then he didn't feel safe getting up just yet. His eyes shifted to the clothes hamper next to his nightstand; there, draped across the top, was his towel from his shower earlier that night. Brian leaned forward and strained, his fingers only brushing the terrycloth material at first, but finally, he grasped it and pulled it toward him with relief.

Once he was cleaned up he stood, his knees and hips hurting. Brian looked down into the garbage at what appeared to be red and yellow mucus. Was that blood mixed in with what could only be his diarrhea?

Suddenly, Brian was overcome with vertigo. He broke out in a profuse sweat, and his body began to sway back and forth. After a moment he collapsed, falling back onto his mattress without a care in the world.

Brian Olson was passed out cold, half-naked, in his own feverish sweat.

∞

Kathy Olson woke with a start to the incessant sound of the beeping alarm next to her head. What day was it? Friday? No, Saturday. Why the heck had she turned the damn thing on, anyway? Then she remembered: she and Brian were supposed to visit her brother Rich and his wife Deanne. It would be a chance for Brian to play with his cousins, Micki and Mandy before school started on Monday.

She sat up on the edge of her bed and put her head in her hands, waiting for the tired cobwebs to clear from her brain. Would Brian be up? She glanced at the clock once more: seven-thirty-two. Of course not; what was she thinking.

After several minutes Kathy stood and staggered to her bathroom. There, she brushed her teeth and combed her hair. She returned to her bedroom and put on a pair of her favorite jeans and an old Denver Broncos sweatshirt, as well as a pair of bootie socks, before heading to the kitchen. She desperately needed coffee, and she knew it.

As soon as she opened her bedroom door, the stink hit her: a vile odor reeking of rotten bowels, as far as she was concerned. Her hand went right to her nose and mouth in an effort to protect them, and she even had to squint her eyes because the stench was causing them to burn.

"Holy heck?" She mumbled through her fingers. Kathy looked down the hall and saw nothing but stillness and peace. "Brian!"

There was no response.

She crossed the hall, her hand still over her mouth, and knocked hard on her son's bedroom door. "Brian!" She listened only for a second, then quickly took her hand off her mouth to yell once again. She replaced it just as fast; the smell was simply disgusting.

With a quick turn of the knob, she opened Brian's bedroom door. It took her only a second of looking, but she knew almost immediately that her son was not in his room. The smell was really strong in there, so she proceeded forward.

Next to his bed was his trash bin. She stooped and looked inside, and immediately her gag reflex took over. His wastebasket was filled with what looked like bloody puke, but it smelled like rotten crap. Kathy fell back off her feet and landed hard on her backside before flipping over and trying to crawl out of the room with her hand still over her face.

Once in the hall, she got to her feet and ran for the front door. Grabbing the key off of the hook and undoing the double deadbolt in a flash, Kathy flung it open and ran outside, where she promptly got sick in the bushes, throwing up a bit of mucus and water before dry heaving for a bit. Afterward, she put her hands on her knees and stood, bent over, just trying to catch her breath.

Where the heck was Brian? Had he actually defecated in his garbage can? Or had he vomited?

She stood upright and looked back toward her house, which sat still and peaceful before her. Her mind was spinning; Lord, she hadn't even had her coffee! Had her son gotten sick and tried to walk to the hospital? He'd better be sick, she thought, or I'm going to kick his butt for making such an awful mess.

Suddenly, there was a crash from inside the house. Kathy jerked to attention and listened carefully. It was followed by very intentional shuffling, but nothing came into her view through the opened door. She felt confused, and even a bit relieved.

"Brian?"

She stepped back into the house taking her time to secure the deadbolt and call her son's name once again. "Brian? Where are you?"

More shuffling, then a faint voice, "In the laundry room."

She barely recognized his voice, but Kathy wasn't

deterred. Her mother's instincts kicked in right away, and she was off like a shot for the laundry room. He must be trying to wash his clothes, she thought.

As she rounded the corner where the door to the utility area was, she could hear a grunting sound, but the noise didn't register with her. When she came to the doorway she stopped cold, and an icy hand of terror gripped her heart. Brian stood before her, but it really wasn't Brian.

His flesh was a deep gray, and it was ragged and bruised at many places. His entire left cheek looked as if it had been torn from his face, leaving a gaping hole where Kathy could see his teeth and tongue clearly. But regardless of all this, most terrible of all, Brian was smiling at her, and he looked more than happy to see her at that specific moment in time.

Kathy's mouth dropped open, and she took a step back, more out of reflex than fear. But it didn't take long for that old friend, Fear, to take over, and that was the exact moment at which panic set in for her. She went into shock almost immediately.

Brian, her beloved baby boy, her best friend, and the young man she had been raising so diligently and properly wanted to eat her. Of that, Kathy Olson was positive. She stumbled and tried to get on all fours so she could get away from the monster before her.

"Brian!" Kathy screamed his name with all her might as she flipped herself over and began clawing at the teal hallway carpet. Her feet moved in perfect harmony with her scrambling hands, but neither could seem to get any kind of grip or footing. Brian's eyes, while dead, were completely alight with the excitement of having prey spread out before him.

He took a single staggering step, and then another, in her direction.

After what seemed like an hour, the thirty-two-year-old mother finally got both her footing and an unstable grasp on the tacky carpeting. She lurched forward just as her teenaged son's fingers brushed against her stocking foot, and she was keenly aware of his fingers there. Even as she scrambled to get away from him she was aware of his touch; it was sickening and petrifying, all at the same time.

Kathy Olson knew that her son Brian was not himself. She couldn't explain it in her desperate mind, not in the few seconds she had to get away. All she knew was that his eyes had been empty during the split second she looked into them. They were still his eyes, but they were empty, and completely void of all life or consciousness.

"Brian!" She was able to pull her legs and feet forward at the very last second, and with that movement, she willed a burst of energy which enabled her to sprint down the hall. Kathy stumbled at first, almost reminiscent of a horror film, but she quickly gained her footing and darted away from him.

His voice was raspy, yet grotesquely wet at the same time. It sounded as though he were trying to scream with a large wad of phlegm in his throat, and regardless of who he had been, she had enough sense and reason to continue to flee. But she could feel him behind her; his presence coming up on her, no matter how lurching and slow, was identical to that of a spirit saturated in a mist of a thousand rainstorms.

She made it, finally, into the hallway, stumbling the entire ten feet. Kathy felt her son's hands more than once, landing on her, grabbing, then losing their grip. She would kick backward at his hands, inciting angrier and angrier growls from his lips.

Her mind was racing as she scrambled to make it to the living room, but everything around her seemed to be going in slow motion, especially her own movement. Much like in a dream, it seemed that her limbs were bogged down in tar, and she thought she would never get away. Why was her son doing this? What had happened to him, to his face and body? From what she could see, Brian looked… dead.

By the time Kathy reached the end of the hallway she was able to glance over her shoulder; Brian was a good five feet behind her. While he was still making his way to her, it appeared that he was struggling terribly to get the job done. He seemed to be walking on the outside of his right foot, and his right leg was turned dramatically inward. Kathy didn't waste any time in getting to her feet fast.

Kathy took a sudden right at the end of the hall and headed for the front door. When she reached it she turned the knob, but it would not open; it was locked tight. In her panicked state, she had completely forgotten the fact that she used a double deadbolt.

Glancing over at the hook. Where were the keys to the deadbolt? She recalled just locking the door minutes before.

Suddenly, Brian was on her, ripping at her shoulders and shirt with unusually strong hands. Kathy turned to the creature who used to be her son and began flailing her arms with all her might. Kathy was a realist and always had been. She knew, without a doubt, that the monster trying to hurt her was not her son, not at all.

At first, she thought she was getting the best of him. After all, he didn't seem to be able to focus his eyes very well, and all he could manage from his mouth were bizarre, wet noises, grunts, and growls. He also seemed to be having a hard time maneuvering on his legs. But when Kathy tried to push him, as unstable as he was, he simply wouldn't fall over, and with each shove, he seemed to get madder and madder, and his rage added to his strength.

She gave him one more shove with all of her might, and he staggered backward for a split second. Kathy grabbed a heavy brass lamp from the end table between the sofa and front door, and with both hands swung the lamp at his head as hard as she could. Its base hit Brian in the skull with a sickening 'CRUNCH!', and he finally toppled over and fell to the floor on his back, his arms and legs working like those of a stranded turtle.

Kathy didn't waste a second. The front door and deadbolt were forgotten, and instead, she ran for the garage entrance, grabbing the keys to her car as she ran past the kitchen counter. Taking only a second to look over her shoulder, she saw that Brian had made it to his hands and knees, and her heart began to pound relentlessly.

Pleading in a trembling voice as she flung open the garage door and ran down the trio of wood steps and to her old sedan. Kathy grabbed the door handle and pulled, but it was locked.

"Damn it!" She screamed. She knew that she had locked it when she last got home, and she was mentally kicking herself, hard. With shaking hands, she found the key to the door and tried to put it into the lock, but she dropped them on the cement floor.

"Aargh!"

Kathy swung her head around to see Brian in the doorway, his hands on both sides of the jamb. Her blood ran cold with horror as she realized that he was smiling. What the heck was going on?

She tried to keep her eyes on him, glancing down only to try to put the key in the door lock again. He was trying to take the steps down, but he seemed to be having trouble mastering them. Tears began to run down her face, and a sob escaped her throat.

"Where do you think you're going, Mother?" he asked her in his wet, guttural voice.

The key finally went in, and as she turned it she screamed, "No! No, Brian! Somebody, please help me!"

The car door came open right away as she pulled the handle, and Kathy tumbled into her seat. Next, she slammed the door and locked it, then reached over and locked the passenger side. When she sat back Brian was at the car window; he ran his wet tongue up and down the length of it, and Kathy began to cry in earnest.

As she tried, through her tears, to get the key into the ignition, Brian walked to the back of the car. She couldn't see what he was doing; the garage was simply too dark. Worst of all, she could barely see to put the key in, due to both the darkness and the tears in her eyes.

Trembling so hard, she dropped the keys two times. The first time she found them easily, but the second time she couldn't track them down. She tried to turn on the dome light, then remembered that it had burned out last week. She felt around her feet and under her seat, but she couldn't feel the keys anywhere.

Suddenly a loud crash came at the driver's side window. Kathy jerked toward it violently only to see a large, circular chip with small breaks webbing out from the center. On the other side stood Brian with a cinder block held over his head. His grin was sick and toothy, and spittle was running down his chin. A flap of flesh hung off his cheek, which seemed to have ripped more, and the sight nearly sent Kathy into shock. She tried to scream again, the keys forgotten, but no sound came out.

He swung the block down toward the window again, breaking it even more. The glass broke inward, bits of it flying into Kathy's mouth and hair. Her hands went to her face and came back down with blood on them.

All at once she remembered: the horn.

She pushed at it, and it gave a brief honk, so she

tried to lean on it. Right then, Brian grabbed his mother by her hair and gave it a yank. She looked up into his yellowed, milky eyes in terror.

"Yum, Mommy," he growled, spit flying. "Yum."

With a single yank, Brian Olson pulled his mother cleanly through her car window and threw her to the hard floor. Her head bounced off it hard, and now dazed, she reached for the spot to rub it. But she never had the chance to do much more.

Brian straddled her and sat on her midsection. Grabbing her hair once more, he jerked her head back, exposing her neck. Leaning forward, he sank his teeth into her flesh. Blood shot from her neck and immediately began to pool on the floor beneath her. Kathy's eyes went wide with shock, and her body went limp.

Her son sat up, skin and part of a vein hanging from his mouth. He chewed with a sober look on his dead face. As Kathy bled out, her body twitched beneath him, but he took no notice. "Yum…"

CHAPTER 6

Michelle and Megan sat in the Intensive Care Unit waiting room, both of them on the edge of their seats. They had been back at Suburban Medical Center for more than a half-hour, and as of yet, they had not been permitted to enter Melanie's room until the doctor had a word with Michelle. Unfortunately, no doctor had approached them, and the mother in her was becoming very impatient.

According to the nurses at the desk, Melanie's pediatrician, Dr. Diana Moss, had been called, and she was currently meeting with Dr. Hilliard regarding Melanie's condition. While Michelle was no doctor or hospital employee, she thought this was odd; never before when one of the girls had a medical emergency had Dr. Moss been called in for consultation. Usually, a report was sent to her, which she would refer to during their follow-up checkup.

Michelle stood up and began to pace around. Megan glanced up at her mother from her tablet but quickly looked back down. She was as worried as Michelle. Not because of doctors meeting and such, but only because she had a really bad feeling in her stomach. Nothing seemed right about Mel getting sick, and for some reason, Megan thought that maybe Mel might not... get better.

"Mrs. Casperson?"

Michelle and Megan both looked up to the direction the voice was coming from. It was Dr. Hilliard, and beside him stood Dr. Moss. Dr. Moss was smiling, but it didn't touch her eyes, and both of the Caspersons' took note of that fact. They rushed to the doctors to hear the verdict.

"How's Mel?" Michelle asked anxiously.

Dr. Hilliard took her by the arm. "Let's all sit down, shall we?"

"I don't want to sit down," she said sternly. "How's Melanie?"

Dr. Moss reached out and touched Michelle's arm. "We don't have to sit if you don't want to. Michelle, it seems there is an issue with Melanie's blood work, and as of yet we cannot explain it, but we are working on it."

"Issue?" she asked. "What kind of issue?"

Dr. Moss looked up at Hilliard, and he took over. "Something... unidentifiable... has taken up residence in her bloodstream. Now, it isn't a virus, and it isn't bacteria, at least not like any we have ever seen. We are working to identify it so we can remedy it faster, and in the meantime, we are working on stopping it. The issue is that it seems to be taking over Melanie's body one organ at a time, and at a very rapid pace."

Michelle just looked back and forth between the two physicians, her mouth open and her eyes confused. "So, what is it doing to her organs, then?"

"Well, that's the difficult part to explain," Dr. Moss said.

"What do you mean?"

Dr. Hilliard took over once again. "It seems to be shutting them down, but her heart is beating, and her body is functioning, even though it should not be. Melanie is alive, Mrs. Casperson, but we have no idea why."

"She woke up at one point, Michelle, and she became intensely violent, even biting one of the nurses, Julie Yates, to the point of drawing blood," Dr. Moss finished.

As if in a trance, Michelle shuffled over to one of the waiting room chairs and plopped down hard. She simply couldn't comprehend what they were saying to her. Her daughter was alive, but she should be dead? What the heck did that mean, anyway?

She felt the comforting hand of Megan stroking her arm, and she glanced over at the girl, who looked as confused and worried as she felt.

"Michelle?"

She looked up to see both doctors sitting across from them. When had they sat down? She didn't even recall them approaching.

"Yes?"

"We need to know if Melanie has come into any kind of contact with anything out of the ordinary in the last week," Dr. Hilliard explained. "Anything… food, beverages, cleaning supplies, chemicals… anything at all."

Michelle tried to think, but her mind was in such a jumble that she could sort out nothing that made any sense. Both of her daughters had done their usual activities, eaten the normal foods, and played their typical games. She just couldn't pinpoint anything.

"The pen," Megan stated matter-of-factly.

All three adults looked at Megan. The girl looked crazy-calm, but her eyes were wide, and the look on her face said 'Of course!' Michelle began to nod frantically.

"What pen, Megan?" Dr. Moss asked.

The girl sat forward in her chair and began to speak quickly. "Mom bought us a couple of those new Lumiosa pens for school. You know, the ones that write in ink that looks like a hologram? I wouldn't have thought of it, but after dinner the other night I was reading the back of the package because I wanted to see what the ink was made of…"

"What did it say?"

Megan's face scrunched up as if she were trying to remember. "There was a warning. Something about 'Don't touch the ink until it is dry.' To me, it was funny that they made that into a warning, because the only reason it said not to touch it was because it would smear, and that was stupid. No other pen does that, and they all smear."

Dr. Hilliard jumped up. "It may be a long shot, but we need one of those pens; where did you purchase it?"

"Mom took us to Community Rexall here in Thornton," she replied.

Michelle nodded vigorously, though she was still in a bit of a daze. "Yes. Community Rexall."

Diana took off running down the hall, and Dr. Hilliard said, "You can see Melanie if you like, but I want you to be prepared—she is not herself. She looks pretty bad, and she is currently strapped down for her own safety and the safety of those around her. I'm afraid I'll have to insist that you stay at least two feet from her bed at all times, okay?"

Michelle nodded, and she and Megan followed Dr. Hilliard to Melanie's room.

R.W.K. Clark

CHAPTER 7

Paige Daugherty ambled up the sidewalk to Kathy Olson's front door. The two of them were supposed to do some grocery shopping and have lunch together, and now it was nearly eleven o'clock. She had gotten no word from her neighbor, which was very unusual. Kathy was one of the most responsible and timely women Paige knew.

The house seemed deathly quiet. The front door was locked, as usual. What was out of the ordinary, on a breezy, cool day like this Kathy would always have the windows open to let the air inside, but today they were closed. Paige rang the bell a couple of times and waited, then she took note of the newspaper on the stoop.

"Kathy?" She peeked through the front window, but the shades were drawn. "Kath? It's Paige. We should get going! Are you okay?"

She stepped away from the door and decided to walk around the house. Something inside of her felt nervous and uneasy. She thought it was playing out a lot like an episode of 'Real Crime,' and she didn't like the taste it left in her mouth.

Paige walked around to the side and tried the gate to

the privacy fence, but it was locked tight; so much for going to the back door. On tiptoes, she tried to peek through the window there, which would have been Kathy's room, but she just couldn't reach. Maybe she should get something from the other side to stand on, like the garbage bin.

She walked around to the other side of the house, crossing the driveway as she went. Along that side of the house, she saw no garbage bin, which led her to believe that Kathy had put it into the garage, but the central air unit was there, and it was directly beneath a window.

Paige climbed up on top of it and looked into the window to see Brian's room. It was messy, just as any teenage boy's room would be. The bed was unmade, and a garbage bin sat next to it, as if he had perhaps been sick. She found herself wondering if maybe Kathy had to take Brian to the hospital or something.

She decided to leave a short note in the front screen door to let Kathy know she had been there, and that she was concerned. She began to fish around in her shoulder bag for a notepad and pen as she walked back to the front door. Paige was just crossing the driveway when something caught her eye.

Running slowly out from under the garage door was a pool of blood.

"Oh my…!"

Now Paige's heart began to beat out of control. She took her cell phone from her purse and attempted to dial 911, but she was getting no signal. Instead, she began to pound madly on the garage door, screaming both Kathy and Brian's names as she did so. Within only seconds the garage door began to open slowly on its tracks.

Paige stopped her screaming and watched as the door lifted. "Kathy?" she said. When the door was high enough she saw that the puddle of blood stood alone; there was no one lying there, hurt or otherwise. What the heck was going on?

Without a second thought, she stepped into the garage and crossed it, taking immediate notice of the broken car window. The next thing she noticed was that the door into the house was wide open, so she headed for it, calling out for her friend and her friend's son all the while.

Paige stepped into the kitchen slowly, a sinking feeling in her stomach. "Kathy! It's Paige! Are you okay?"

Nothing looked out of the ordinary in the house at all. There were a couple of small messes, and there was a horrible stench that was nearly unbearable, but everything else looked okay. But when she got to the living room and saw the lamp on the floor, she knew everything was not okay.

That was when she heard the shuffling, the uneven, dragging shuffling of feet which sounded as though it was coming from someone who was either drunk or handicapped. Paige spun around and immediately took a sharp breath. Her mind began to race as she processed what she saw.

There stood Brian; he was standing still, just watching her. Kathy was slowly coming up behind him, and it looked to Paige like her friend was struggling to walk. Both of them looked pale gray, and Brian even had a tear in his cheek that seemed to allow her a complete view of the inside of his mouth. Kathy was missing part of her neck, and her shirt was completely blood-soaked, with bits and pieces of what appeared to be tissue on it.

"Paige," Kathy gurgled as she reached out for her, making her way to the more-than-welcome guest.

Paige began to back toward the front door, her hand behind her groping blindly for the knob. When she got hold of it, she turned around and tried desperately to open the door, but to no avail. Soon, she turned back around to head for the rear door, but Kathy and Brian were already upon her.

Paige screamed and cried, clawing at the door, the floor, and at both Kathy and Brian. They had cornered her, and as Brian tore into the flesh of her stomach and Kathy ripped at her nose with her teeth, the last thing in Paige's mind was, 'You are both going to go to jail for this.'

CHAPTER 8

While Diana left Suburban Medical Center to purchase an Aspen Lumiosa, Dr. Hilliard escorted both Michelle and Megan down the long hallway in Intensive Care to see Melanie. He was filled with apprehension and dread, but the girl was strapped down, and it was imperative that her mother and sister see her. After all, the girl was already dead; every test said so.

Dr. Hilliard's fear was based on what had happened earlier. Little Melanie Casperson had been lying on the hospital bed, her eyes closed and her breathing shallow, and nurse Julie Yates had been adjusting the tubing to her saline IV. Suddenly, in front of everyone, the child's eyes had opened, and she had grabbed the woman's arm and sunk her teeth into it. Blood had sprayed in all directions. In all of his years practicing medicine, Dr. Hilliard had never really witnessed anything like it.

The thoughts in his head reminded him to check on Miss Yates' welfare. He approached the girl's hospital room with the Caspersons' and pushed the thoughts from his mind. Weighing his words carefully, he turned to Michelle.

"Now, Mrs. Casperson, I cannot emphasize enough

that you must stay away from her bedside until we are able to figure out exactly what has happened to her and how it can be rectified, do you understand?" Hilliard asked.

Michelle nodded at him, but she never took her eyes from the door to the room. He knew in his soul that she was only appeasing him with her nodding, and the knowledge nagged at him. He glanced at Megan; she had a very worried look in her eyes, and she kept shifting them to her inattentive mother.

Hilliard finally grabbed the handle and gave it a yank, opening the door with his shoulder as he did so. Melanie was lying in bed, small and extremely pale. So pale, in fact, that her skin was a grayish-white, almost giving her the appearance of a corpse. Her eyes were closed, and her breathing was ragged. She looked dead, but all Michelle saw was her baby girl.

She began to walk over to her daughter right away, and Dr. Hilliard grabbed her by the arm once again. "Mrs. Casperson, you have to keep back, okay?"

She looked at him blankly and gave him another nod before continuing. She did stop about two-and-a-half feet from the bed, and both the doctor and Megan saw the tears falling down her mother's face.

"Melly?" she said in a light voice, but with a low tone.

Megan was afraid, and she was afraid to her core. Something inside of her screamed to stay away from her little sister. She felt bad about it in her head, but the voice of her heart was louder, and it was that voice she chose to listen to.

Her mother stepped forward a couple of inches. "Melanie?"

Megan reached out, trembling, and took hold of the hem of Dr. Hilliard's white coat. The man glanced down at the girl and felt a chill go up his spine; she looked petrified, and from what he knew so far, rightly so. For all intents and purposes, the sick little girl on the bed was nothing more than a monster, and he knew it.

"Michelle," he asked with a bit of trepidation. "Are you going to be okay for a bit? I'm going to go grab the nurse so we can do a vital check on her and go over a tentative treatment plan."

She nodded, once again not looking at him or even toward him. Hilliard stepped forward and took her by the arm. "Michelle, I have to know that you will follow the instructions, or I cannot let you visit her."

She shot him a look that should have left him on the floor, sore and bleeding. "Of course, Doctor," she almost spat.

He turned to Megan. "Try to keep her back honey. Okay?"

The girl gave him a nod, and he left the room. He was going to touch base with the nurses about Melanie, but he also wanted to check on Julie Yates. He didn't know if Melanie's condition was contagious or not, but it was best to find out sooner than later.

∞

Diana stepped off the elevator, a plastic bag in her hand. Inside was one of the Aspen Lumiosa pens; she was headed to the lab to have some of the ink analyzed, if at all possible. The fact of the matter was that she had no idea what she was looking for, and neither would the lab.

Her short heels clattered on the cold tile as she headed toward the hospital laboratory. It was located in the basement, and there was always a constant chill there, but today Diana had a feeling that her goosebumps had more to do with little Melanie Casperson than they did the temperature. She shook it off and continued on.

When she walked through the main door to the laboratory area the first person she saw was exactly who she was looking for: Roy Fitch. Roy was one of the best lab men in Colorado. She had gone to college with him before transferring to medical school, and the two got along very well. He would make time for her testing, and she knew it, no matter how overwhelmed with work he might be.

Roy looked up, and a large smile came over his face. "Diana! You're never in the hospital anymore! What brings you?"

"Hi, Roy," she replied in a friendly voice. "No, I'm not here much since I opened my practice, but I have a patient here today, and something of an emergency has come up with their case."

Roy knit his brow. "What do you mean?"

She proceeded to explain to him the situation with little Melanie, including with emphasis on how the child seemed to be dead already. "The only thing her family can pinpoint that she came into contact with is ink from a new pen." Diana pulled the pen out of the bag. "Her sister, Megan, told me that there was a warning on the package, which sounded strange. I went and picked one up, and sure enough, here it is."

Diana handed the pen to Roy, and he immediately flipped over the cardboard and scanned it with his eyes. "Warning," he said. "Do not touch ink when wet; highly smearable. Why would they even put that on there? All ink smears."

"I know; it's almost like a distraction. Like they are trying to cover their butts." She paused and let her words sink in. "I need you to test the ink for me and tell me what it consists of. I need to know if there is anything in it that could cause the kind of damage we are seeing in Melanie."

Roy glanced around at his workstation, but only briefly. "Absolutely. I'll get on it right now."

"Thank you," she replied, the relief in her voice evident. "And Roy, if you find anything unusual will you introduce it to some biologic? I want to know how it reacts to life in general."

"Already thought of," he replied as he began to tear the package open.

Diana turned to go. "I'm heading back to my patient, so just page me when and if you find anything, okay?"

"You've got it."

With that, Diana left the lab and headed back to the ICU as quickly as her feet, and the elevator would carry her.

CHAPTER 9

The afternoon had come and gone, and now it was fast approaching evening.

Paige Daugherty reached up with a flat palm and slapped the button on the garage wall. Slowly the garage door began to open once again. She didn't remember how it got closed, or even coming through it when she did. Heck, she didn't even know her name.

She began to lurch toward the still-opening door, one shoe off and one shoe on. Paige was torn up, both literally and figuratively. Brian and Kathy had managed to put her through the wringer, but as soon as she went through her transformation and began fighting back, the two of them eased up. She decided it was time to leave. She was hungry, and it almost felt as if the hunger wouldn't wait.

As she walked, she stepped in the congealed blood on the floor with her barefoot, and each step after that managed to leave a clear bloody footprint. Paige took no notice of any of that; not the jelly-like blood between her toes, not the metallic scent of it, nothing. All she could smell was fresh, wholesome blood, and it seemed that the aroma of it was surrounding her.

Once she was out in the late evening setting sun, she raised her head to the sky and attempted to look into the sun itself. It seemed so easy; she didn't flinch or squint at all. It seemed that her eyes were able to handle its brightness without a problem, even though she couldn't really see anything very clearly at all.

Paige could hear the voices and laughter of children, and her mouth began to water. She looked around once again, but she could see no one. Even though she was quite dead, it seemed she was still able to think fairly well. She thought of her home and decided that was where she would go. She would have something to drink, some icy water, and then she would go back out and find where the laughter was coming from.

She began to lurch once again, heading determinedly in the direction of her house. Suddenly, from behind her, she heard a throaty growl, and she stopped long enough to turn and see what it was. There were Kathy and Brian, and they were both following her. It seemed like they thought it was best to start moving as well.

Paige tried her front door, but it wouldn't open. Of course, she had locked it when she left, and now she had neither purse nor keys. She remembered none of this, but that didn't stop her progress. With a single swing of her wrist, she broke the window which ran alongside the door. Then, as easy as could be, she reached through it and unlocked the door. Brian and Kathy got to her step just as she entered, and they joined her.

There were only two things she was aware of: her

insatiable hunger and the incessant thirst. She would tend to the hunger in a bit, but at that moment the only thing she could think of was water. Paige struggled to the kitchen with both of the Olsons' on her heels. All three of them grunted and groaned as if pained and exhausted, but they felt none of that.

Paige's coordination was all but gone, with the exception of her ability to walk. Her eyesight was gloomy and shadowy, but she could make out the dish drainer and just barely recognize a large plastic tumbler, which she had just placed there that morning. She reached out for it, but was having a heck of a time getting her hand to go where she wanted it to. She swung it back and forth in her efforts, knocking things here and there and sending them flying.

Finally, she got her hand on the tumbler, which had fallen over on its side noisily. With one hand steadying herself with the kitchen counter she staggered along it, and when she got to the sink, she clumsily turned on the cold water full blast. Once she was able to line up the glass with the water, she quickly filled it and put it to her face, splashing herself sloppily as she did so.

For the most part, Paige got a pretty hefty drink. She started to attempt to refill the vessel, but Brian suddenly snatched the tumbler from her hand, and now he, too, filled it with the water, which continued to pour from the tap. Kathy was behind them both, growling loudly and with anger; she was also terribly thirsty.

"Paige!" The voice came from behind them all. Brian and Kathy, who had been fighting over the empty glass by that point, dropped it to the floor and tried to turn to see who was there. Paige, on the other hand, turned surprisingly fast, and with sudden grace.

It was Max Fisher, a neighbor man whom Paige had been sleeping with for the last six months. As soon as she saw him a smile came to her face. The other two didn't miss a beat; they started to head for the shocked man right away.

"No!" Paige suddenly gurgled in a lousy attempt to scream. "Mine!" She tried to grab hold of Brian by the shoulder, but the boy was far stronger, and he flung her easily to the floor. Max stepped forward protectively, but the move was out of sheer habit. He knew something was very wrong in Paige Daugherty's house. As soon as he stepped forward, he changed his mind and went into reverse. His backside hit the edge of the dining room table.

He tried to maneuver around the solid oak piece, but there was little room along either side for a man to fit through. Brian reached him first, and he was quickly joined by his mother. Both of them took Max to the floor easily and began to tear into him with wet, terrible noises.

The last thing Max registered was Paige, crawling almost lazily, up the middle and between the two who were already ravaging him. She looked at him, her smile bloody and dead. He knew she was preparing to join them, and his head couldn't wrap around what was happening.

"Max," she purred in her hoarse voice. "Mine…"

CHAPTER 10

Dr. Kyle Hilliard left Melanie Casperson's room in the ICU with much apprehension; he just didn't feel confident that her mother would obey his instructions to stay back from the child's bedside.

Regardless of that fact, he had to go about his own work, so he did so praying that the woman would do as he asked.

Now he needed to go to the nurses' station; there he would see how the girl's vitals had been since his last order, which consisted of her being hooked up to automatic monitors for her vitals, because he didn't trust her in the state she was in to allow the nurses to conduct regular checks. The last actual reported check which he had been aware of had been bad: a barely audible heartbeat, no detectable pulse, and extremely shallow respiration. According to the numbers, the girl should be dead.

It was directly after that check that she had attacked Julie Yates viciously, biting the woman.

He approached the station and beckoned to a nurse named Candace Reilly. She was at the end of the station typing something furiously on her computer keyboard, and she had a sick look on her face. Hilliard felt instant concern, and fear put a metallic taste in his mouth.

"Candace, how are the Casperson girl's vitals?" he asked.

The nurse's eyes shifted. "Um, I'm afraid to go in, but I last checked them about ten minutes ago." She fished a scrap of paper out of her smock pocket, then smirked and tossed the blank scrap onto the desktop. "Nothing. She is flat on everything. Guess I don't need a piece of paper to tell you that."

"I think I should go in and get her visitors," he said thoughtfully. "I can pronounce her, and they can begin to say their goodbyes."

Candace shook her head. "No, you can't. She was wide awake the entire time I was checking the machine, Doctor."

Hilliard glanced over his shoulder. "Listen, I've been so busy I still need to check on Julie Yates. I want you to keep an eye on the girl's room. Call me immediately if anything is going on, and I will go in there as soon as I am done with Julie. Then I'm going to see if the girl is possibly deceased, and we just missed it. This has been crazy from the start."

"I can tell you that Julie is in the same state, Doctor," Candace said as she clamped her eyes shut, as though holding back tears.

"What do you mean?"

Candace shrugged, and tears escaped down her cheeks. "They no sooner had her in a room to be stitched up than she became extremely combative. She was attempting to bite the nurses, and she had to be restrained also. As far as I know, she wasn't able to actually hurt anyone, but everyone is afraid to proceed. We were just waiting for you to be finished to find out what you wanted us to do."

"What room is she in?" he asked.

Candace glanced down the hallway. "Five seventy-two."

Kyle Hilliard didn't miss a beat. He muttered a thank-you to the frightened young nurse and left right away in the direction of the room Julie Yates was in. As he approached, he saw two other nurses standing outside the door talking. One was in tears, her shoulders heaving from her crying. Hilliard could also hear a terrible yelling from inside the room which sounded far more animal than human.

"What's going on with Nurse Yates?" he asked as he approached.

The nurse with a calmer demeanor spoke first. "She is restrained, and we tried to sedate her, but it had no effect, Doctor."

"What did she do to warrant these decisions?"

The nurse, whose tag read 'Carla Bond, RN,' continued. "We were attempting to give her a local. At first, she was cooperative, but then she seemed to pass out. I thought it was from the local, you know, that maybe the needle, or the pain from it. I even thought that perhaps she was just in some kind of shock from the confrontation with the patient who bit her, but..." Her voice trailed off.

Hilliard pressed Carla Bond. "And?"

"Well, all of a sudden her eyes opened up, and she started to kick and fight."

The second nurse, Denise Fletcher, blew her nose on a tissue which she had pulled out of her smock. "She was strong, so strong," she said. "I took hold of her wrists, and she began to try to bite me. I struggled and fought back while Carla strapped her legs, but she was wearing me out."

"Did she manage to hurt you at all? Even the slightest scratch?" he asked.

Denise shook her head. "Nothing. But her eyes, they were so blank, almost like it wasn't Julie in there at all."

The screaming from the other side of the door had subsided while Hilliard and the two nurses spoke. Her presence even slipped their minds a bit, when suddenly the curtain over the window to the room, which blocked the view from the hallway, was thrown open, and Julie Yates stood pounding violently on the thick glass. Spittle flew from her mouth and splattered against the window as she screamed.

Hilliard and the nurses both jumped back, startled. He took one look at Julie, and his heart sank. She was a purplish-gray in color, with dark circles under her eyes. Milky, cataract-type clouds were forming over her eyes, and Kyle Hilliard thought he could almost see her veins through the flesh on her face.

As a doctor, he knew beyond a shadow of a doubt that the woman was dead.

He flew forward and grabbed hold of the door

handle, then leaned backward with all his weight to keep it closed. "Call for help!" he told the nurses. "We need security to bring a master key to this room right away!"

Denise Fletcher was gone in a flash, while Carla Bond came forward to help him in holding the door closed. As soon as Julie Yates saw them, she seemed to figure out what they were doing, and she disappeared behind the door. Within seconds she began to pull violently on the door, trying her best and giving it her all to get out of the room.

"Hurry!" Hilliard yelled at Fletcher at the top of his lungs. He turned to Carla. "We can't let her get out of this room!"

Both of them could tell by her strength alone that there might very well be nothing they could do about it at all.

∞

Diana dropped off the pen in the hospital lab and then made a beeline for the staff lounge on the first floor. She needed to call her answering service and get any messages. It was late Saturday, and she was pretty sure she would be back in the office by tomorrow. At least, she would if they could narrow down the cause of Melanie Casperson's illness.

When she was finished with her calls, she proceeded to the cafeteria. With her salad in hand, she made her way to a table in the corner of the nearly-empty cafeteria. Once she had put the dressing on her greens she began to eat, and only then did she let her mind wander back to the Casperson case. She had never heard of such a crazy thing as pen ink infecting a human being, but she knew that with all the insane things going on in the world she shouldn't be surprised by anything anymore.

Suddenly, Diana's own children came to her mind. She had two: Todd was a junior in high school, and Emma, a freshman. Her heart began to pound hard when she thought of them. It wasn't Todd she was worried about; he was a jock with nothing more on his mind than football and girls. But Emma was the artistic one, the one who was always keeping her eye out for creative new supplies and art equipment.

Diana had made them both get their own supplies that year.

She dropped her fork and dialed Emma's cell phone; her daughter answered on the second ring.

"'Hello?"

Diana breathed a sigh of relief. "Emma, are you feeling okay?"

"Mom?" the girl replied. "Of course I am. What's up?"

"Listen, when you went for your supplies did you happen to buy one of those Lumiosa pens?" she asked.

"Oh, yeah!" her daughter's voice got excited. "Those are so cool! I haven't used it yet, though. I'm waiting for classes to start. Those things are expensive. Did you know—"

Diana was sitting up straight in her chair now, feeling a mix of massive relief and terrible tension. "Yes, they're expensive," she replied. "Listen to me, there is some bad news about the pens. They are making kids very, very sick. I want you to throw it away, do you hear me?"

"What? Throw it away?"

Now she began to get frustrated. She hated when her children argued with her. "Yes, Emma! Throw it away now! Do as I say, and I'll explain when I get home!"

Emma was quiet for a moment. "Okay, okay. I'll throw it away."

Diana let out another sigh of relief. "I'll give you the money you spent on it, okay? Listen, I love you very much."

"I love you too, Mom."

She disconnected from Emma and picked up her fork just as her pager went off. She glanced down to see that it was from the lab, and immediately she began to tremble. Why was she so nervous? Regardless of what was going on, they would be able to fix it. She glanced at her watch and found herself surprised; it had only been just over four hours since she dropped the pen off to Roy Fitch.

Diana gave up on her salad and put her tray on the conveyor belt which led to the dishwashing area. She then began to walk to the elevator; she thought about calling Roy, but then thought better of it. She would be there in less than a minute; it could wait that long.

The ride down to the basement took only a couple of minutes, and soon she was walking through the lab door.

"Hey, Roy," she said. "So, I take it you have something for me?"

He looked up, and the first thing Diana noticed was how serious his face was. Roy glanced quickly around the lab, and when he saw that two other workers were present, he snatched up a thin manila folder and gestured with his thumb.

"How about we talk in my office?" he asked.

Diana's smile fled from her face. "Sure," she replied, following his lead.

Once inside he shut the door, then turned to her. "Yes, I found something, and it wasn't hard to pinpoint."

She sat in a cushioned chair across from his desk, which he was making his way to. "What do you have, Roy?"

"I'm not sure, but I can tell you that it's not good." The man sat down and put the folder on the blotter in front of him. "The pen's ink is comprised of a chemical I have personally neither encountered nor heard of. While I can't say for sure, I am willing to bet that it is this chemical that gives the ink its three-dimensional appearance."

Diana knit her brow. "And that is bad how?"

Roy shrugged his shoulders. "Well, that's not bad, in and of itself. It's what happened when I introduced it to both human blood and tissue that I consider bad."

Now Diana felt her blood run cold, and goosebumps rose on her flesh. "Just lay it on the line, Roy. If the problem is serious enough, we need to get on a solution right away, and I am convinced that it is, from what I am seeing in my patient."

"First, I introduced a human blood sample," he continued. "My own, to be exact. Immediately it began to… kill… the sample. Now, bleach will do that, as you know, so I didn't freak out too much. But then I introduced a skin sample and a pretty significant one at that."

"Hopefully not one of your own?"

He held up a bandaged finger. "Once I observed how it treated the blood I didn't think twice."

She continued to stare at him. "So?"

"Not only did it cause immediate severe damage to the tissue, but it also began to bond to it almost right away." He paused and began to fidget. "It 'died,' I guess you could say, but then it sort of… came back to life. The issue here is that the tissue was literally dead; there was nothing good, or really living, left in it."

Diana just stared at him and let his words sink in. She turned what he had just told her over and over in her mind, but she could make no sense of anything he said. Roy watched her, waiting for her to say something, but when it became apparent that she was at a loss, he continued once again.

"I guess what I am saying is, in the case of a living human, if this compound were introduced through broken skin—say a cut or a scrape—it would cause instant death, without letting the subject die."

Now Diana stood up, her mind racing and her stomach sick. "What about their mind?"

"Well, it's going to spread as fast as the heart beats," he said in a low voice. "The victim is going to die, their personal awareness will cease. I'll have to do further tests, but I'm willing to say they would become violent, if not a vegetable. But I repeat, I can't be sure." He cleared his throat. "What about your patient? What is their state?"

Diana opened the door to his office to leave, turning back to him for only a second. "We have a serious problem on our hands, Roy. Will you keep working on it?"

"I'll do what I can," he replied, standing immediately.

Diana left his office, a jumble of emotions coursing through her, the first of which was panic. They had a mess on their hands. Hopefully, this was something that could be rectified quickly.

The first thing that had to be done was to demand that Aspen conduct an immediate recall on the Lumiosa. "I will be in the staff lounge making some calls if you need me."

CHAPTER 11

Randy was lying in bed, staring at the ceiling in the dim light which managed to seep through the blinds in his bedroom. It was early Sunday morning; his wife, Charlotte, always rose early, regardless of the day. She would be downstairs, making his coffee and reading the paper. In about an hour she would begin making breakfast for their two boys, Jeremy and Jason. On Monday the boys would return to school, Jeremy in the second grade and Jason in the first. Charlotte had started getting them out of bed early a month ago to get them ready for the school year schedule.

He thought about his confrontation with Roger McGinley, which had resulted in his firing. He had gathered his belongings and been out of there in fifteen minutes flat, but only because McGinley had sent security down to escort him out of the building. He had no time to copy computer files to his thumb drive or his personal cloud service, and as a result, he had hardly gotten a wink of sleep since.

He planned to take care of that today. After breakfast, he was going to go to Aspen with the employee key he had copied ten years ago, sneak into the building and get those files. Then he was going to go the extra mile: he was going to set fire to each and every rat cage in the lab.

They would burn up before the sprinklers had a chance to put them out; he would see to it. He would saturate them in gasoline, and he would drop a match right into it. The thought of making all of this mess right brought a smile to his face.

How the heck was McGinley covering up his findings? He couldn't begin to imagine, but he was going to expose that man if it was the last thing he did. Randy simply couldn't imagine what the effect of the ink would be on humans, but if it was anything like the lab rats, well…

He sat up on the edge of the bed and stretched, then stood and headed for the shower. He was so relieved by his plan that he was able to sing as he washed, and that was a good feeling. Within a half-hour's time, he was trotting downstairs to get some coffee and breakfast, clean, dressed, and still humming.

Charlotte looked up at him from the table, her coffee cup halfway to her mouth. "You're in a good mood this morning! Nice to see!"

"Yes, I am," he replied as he filled his own mug. He walked to the table and bent down to kiss his wife. "Listen, I have some running to do this morning, so I'm going to skip breakfast."

She looked up from the paper. "Fine. What's up?"

Randy sat down and took a sip of his coffee. Shrugging, he replied, "I just forgot a couple of things at the office. Won't take me long. When I get back, I thought we could go have lunch at your mother's."

Charlotte looked at him as though he had grown an arm out of his forehead. "If I didn't know better, I would think you are sick, but I'm not going to look a gift horse in the mouth. She'll love the company. Thanks, dear."

Randy nodded and took the sports section from the paper. He wasn't much of a fan of any sports, but he always read up on them on Sunday, just to keep up with the guys at work. The thought made him smile; he didn't have any *guys at work* anymore.

∞

Ten minutes later Jeremy and Jason appeared, their hair tousled and their eyes tired. "I'm hungry," Jason said as he approached the table, dragging his blanket behind him.

Charlotte stood to prepare some food. "Fine, dear, but the blanket can't be at the table. You know better, Jason."

"I forgot," the boy mumbled as he climbed down and headed to return the blanket.

Randy stopped him as he passed and planted a kiss on his messy hair. "I've got some errands to run," he said, releasing his youngest son. "Had to steal a kiss. You too, Jeremy. Come over here."

"Ugh, Dad," the boy said, faking his disappointment. "I'm too big for kisses."

Randy gave him six kisses and replied, "You are never too big for kisses from Mom and Dad. Got it?"

"Got it."

Charlotte brought two small glasses of orange juice to the table as Randy stood. He embraced her and gave her a kiss as well. "I'm gonna go, dear," he said. "I should be back in an hour or two, okay? Don't forget to call your mom."

"I won't," Charlotte replied. "Drive safe."

Soon, Randy was tooling down the freeway in the direction of Aspen Stationers' Supply. He made only one stop to fill a five-gallon gasoline tank, then resumed his mission. When he pulled up to the gate, he worried about the guard on duty, but only for a brief moment; the weekend guard, Ted, wouldn't know he had been fired. That wasn't something Aspen was too strict on, especially when it came to firings of executives or scientists; they liked to pretend it didn't happen as quickly as possible.

"Dr. Carstens!" Teddy greeted him with a glowing smile. They hadn't seen each other in months, as Randy either stayed all weekend long or didn't come in at all. "How are things going? That new pen of yours is sure doing well! Congrats!"

"Good, Teddy," he replied. "It's going great, and thank you."

The man opened the gate, and Randy drove through, maintaining his calm, cool demeanor. He drove to the rear of the building, where the science and lab employees parked and entered. The lot was empty, much to his relief, and he parked his car right outside the door.

That particular entrance was the only one that didn't require a card in the entire building. Due to Aspen's financial problems it had been swept under the rug when the other doors were converted. That had been the reason Randy had been given a key by upper management, and he had made a copy only because he had a bad habit of losing things. When he left, he had given the original to the security guard who had escorted him out, and he had been so relieved that he had a spare safe at home.

Once he was safe inside, gas can in hand, he made a beeline for his old office. Everything was just as he left it. He glanced around with sadness; he had to admit he would miss this place. But now was not the time for melancholy and tears.

Randy sat at his desk and booted his computer. He had prepared himself in the event that the system wouldn't take his password; it would be simple enough to override. To his surprise his password went right through, granting him complete access. They must have forgotten to take care of the small stuff.

It took him less than fifteen minutes to open the files he needed. It did take a little longer to transfer them to his thumb drive, but he got it done and turned the system off, satisfaction filling his soul and a broad smile on his face. Randy stood and walked to the office door, where he bent down and picked up the gas can. He looked around the room one last time, then shut the light off and left.

The lab door would be locked, but the same key that

got him in the building would get him in the lab. First he tried his code, and of course, it didn't work. They sure didn't forget some things, he thought. He started to dig for his key; then he remembered one of the other scientists, George Keister, had Randy write down his code so he wouldn't forget, and it had been easy: 8765. He punched it in, and the door popped open.

Right away Randy could hear the sickening, abnormal squealing of the rats. The sounds of fighting and ripping flesh were audible as well, and Randy cringed as he fought the urge to gag. He approached the closest cage and peered in.

The two rats were nothing more than dirty, bloody mounds of fur with milky eyes and claws. They were fighting violently, biting and ripping at each other like mad. Randy couldn't tell if they were the same rats, but he guessed they were; they had evolved horrifically. He didn't believe anyone had tended them since he left.

He took his cell phone out of his pocket and began to snap pictures. He took scores of them, from as many angles as possible, then returned his phone to his pocket. Glancing down at the gasoline, Randy began to wonder if he was doing right by killing the rats. Wouldn't that destroy much-needed evidence?

He thought about it for only a minute longer. No, he wouldn't burn down the lab. All of this would not only be evidence, but it might also help authorities to find some kind of antidote or even a preventative vaccine. With that thought Randy found himself wondering if anyone had been affected since the pen's release to the public. He shook his head, as if to shake the thought off of himself, then he picked up the gas and turned to leave.

Roger McGinley stood at the doorway of the lab, leaning against the jamb with his arms crossed over his chest. "What are you doing here?"

Randy's heart began to pound. "I forgot some things in my office, but I realized that none of it was important, so I threw it all away."

"What's the gas for, Randy?" he asked. "And how the heck did you get in the building?"

Randy dodged the last question, preferring to answer the first; hopefully, it would distract the man. "To be honest, I was going to burn the damn place down, but then I decided if there are any negative repercussions from your selfish choices it would be best to let them fall on you."

"Put the gas down."

Randy peered at him in confusion, then set the red gas can on the floor. When he stood, upright Roger was standing there pointing a gun at him casually. He thought he might crap his pants on the spot.

"Move away from it, please," Roger said. "It wouldn't do to kill myself trying to get rid of you."

Randy put his hands in the air and took a few steps forward, putting space between himself and the gasoline. "Look, Roger. I have no interest in bringing you or anyone else down, okay?"

"And I'm supposed to believe that?" The man approached him, clucking his tongue. "Look, I'm sorry that it had to come to this, but I cannot let you sabotage the entire company because you suddenly grew a conscience, do you understand?"

When he got about a foot away from Randy, he cocked the handgun, and his smile grew. Just then a loud screech came from the cage directly behind him, and Roger spun, startled, toward the sound. The gun was no longer pointed at Randy, and he took advantage of the opportunity.

With a single swing, he punched Roger as hard as he could in the side of the head. The man flew backward, dropping the gun, and he fell into the very cage from which the sound had come. It fell off the countertop and clattered to the floor, the lid flying open.

The rats didn't miss a beat; they rushed out of the cage and jumped on Roger McGinley's body, which lay in shock on the floor. Immediately they began to bite him, and he started to scream.

"Randy, what the heck?" he hollered. "Help me! It hurts! Get them off me! Help me!"

Randy stared, as the rats ripped and chewed at the skin on his face with their teeth. He backed away, his mouth hanging open, and thought he might be sick. Suddenly, one of the rats went for the man's neck, and Randy jerked himself out of his trance. He ran out of the lab door and got to his car as quickly as possible.

He sped off the grounds and through the gate, ignoring the wave Teddy gave him. When he was a couple of miles down the road he pulled over, flung his car door open, and vomited all over the pavement. It took him awhile to stop and collect himself, but when he did, he took his cell out of his pocket and dialed 911.

"911 Emergency Response," a woman said. "What is your emergency?"

Randy cleared his throat. "Roger McGinley, president of Aspen Stationers', has just been attacked by some infected rats in the laboratory. They are trying to eat him! Please, hurry! Before they kill him!"

"What is your name, sir?"

"Randy," he replied. "Dr. Randy Carstens. I used to work for Aspen, but I was fired. I came to collect my things, and this took place. I will wait for the ambulance at the main gate if you want."

Randy held the phone to his ear as he turned the car around and headed back for the Aspen building. This was the best way. He could give authorities the information they would need. If he got into trouble, so be it.

After all, he knew in his heart that he deserved it.

R.W.K. Clark

CHAPTER 12

Randy drove back to the main gate of Aspen Stationers' to find Teddy standing in front of the open gate, waving his arms frantically.

"Dr. Carstens, I just got a call in the guard shack from the police station asking about an emergency in the building," Teddy said in high speed, his eyes wide and anxiety-ridden. "Is something wrong inside?"

"Hold on," Randy replied. He pulled his car away from the entrance and parked it before returning to the guard. "Teddy, something pretty unsavory has been going on here, and just now it came to a head. The police and ambulance are on their way, but I think I should wait to fill you in."

Sirens immediately became audible. Even though Teddy could tell how serious Randy was, he asked no further questions. Two EMT vehicles arrived first, and as soon as they pulled up Randy and Teddy jogged up to them. The scientist was extremely happy to see them.

"I'm not sure how to fill you in on all of this," he began, "but there is a heck of a mess inside, and you are going to be in danger by even going in."

Two police cars and a fire truck came racing up to

the gate next, and the first two officers got out of their car and approached Randy and Teddy.

"What is the emergency here, gentlemen?" Asked an officer with a tag on his chest which read 'Bransky.'

Randy cleared his throat. "I'm going to try to fill you in, and it's all going to sound unbelievable, but I promise you that everything I am about to say is the honest truth."

"Is someone in need of medical assistance at this moment?" the cop asked.

Randy held up his hand. "Listen, sir. I am a former lead scientist for Aspen. I was let go last week because of my unwillingness to cover up a volatile situation. The man inside, the man in need of assistance, is currently a direct victim of the situation. I have to say that anyone who comes into contact with him is running a massive risk of becoming the same."

Bransky looked at his partner, a man by the name of Gibbons, with concern. "Go on."

With relief, Randy continued. "We released a new ink pen to the public recently. The Aspen Lumiosa; perhaps you have heard of it?"

Gibbons eyes lit up. "Sure! I bought some for my kids for school!"

"Well, the pens are poisonous," Randy said.

Now Gibbons and Bransky both looked a bit stricken. "What do you mean, 'poisonous'?" Gibbons asked in a low voice.

Randy took a deep breath. "In lab testing the ink from the pens did... horrid things to our lab subjects.

Things that no one could figure out how to stop. I tried to halt the release of the product, but the CEO, Roger McGinley, fired me and released it anyway due to the financial state the company was in."

"If you have been fired, what are you doing here?" Teddy interjected.

Now Randy looked at him, guilt on his face. "I came to download records from my computer to turn over to authorities. Roger caught me, pulled a gun on me, and threatened me with it. But some of the rats got out of the cage when it was knocked over, and they attacked him…"

"Rats attacked Mr. McGinley?" Bransky asked.

Now Randy was getting impatient. Why couldn't they all just let him tell them the story and then decide how to deal with it? All they wanted to do was interrupt and ask stupid questions.

"Listen, these aren't just any rats!" Randy was getting irate. "These rats were the lab subjects for Lumiosa's special ink, and it… it did something to them. They kill each other, but they don't die! They attack, and they eat bites of each other, but the victims, well, they come back to life, and they keep attacking!"

Now Bransky gave a slight chuckle. "What the heck are you talking about?"

Randy could tell this was going to be far more difficult than he initially thought, and if he were they, listening to him, he wouldn't believe it either. "Look, it's this simple. When I left the lab a little while ago, rats were attacking and eating Mr. McGinley. He will need medical attention, but the rats and their condition are infectious. If you go in there you will all need some kind of protection; something to keep them from being able to bite you."

Gibbons spoke up. "You're serious, aren't you?"

"Deadly," Randy replied.

With that, Gibbons didn't wait for another second, even though Bransky maintained his incredulous look. Gibbons turned immediately and made his way over to the EMTs.

"In order to proceed you will need to wear some kind of protective gear," he said. "Do you have anything like that with you in your vehicles?"

While they discussed the situation, Randy turned to Bransky. "Listen, sir. I realize how outlandish this sounds, but who would make something like this up? We need to contact the Feds, the CDC, or someone. The situation needs to be contained as quickly and efficiently as possible, or I promise you, everyone in the country is at risk." He sighed and shook his head. "We already are."

Bransky's smile faded, and he studied Randy with a serious eye. Finally, he took his radio off his hip and spoke into it: "Dispatch, we're going to need Captain Hertz to come to the Aspen Stationers' right away. We have a dangerous situation on our hands."

∞

Roger McGinley's eyes fluttered open.

He had no idea where he was, or even who he was, for that matter. He could see the light coming from above him, and a squealing sound was all around, making his head pound so painfully he thought he would die. It was horrific.

But he didn't need to worry about dying, because Roger McGinley was already dead.

Suddenly he felt a sharp pressure at his calf, then another at his hand. There was no pain, just pressure, and the pressure was very annoying, to say the least. What the heck is that, anyway?

He struggled to sit up, but it seemed that he didn't have the proper motor skills to get the job done easily. McGinley grunted and groaned, spit flying from his mouth. As he tried to control and maneuver his body, he resembled a fish out of the water, flipping and flopping on the floor of the laboratory.

A sharp squealing sound came from his left, and he jerked his head around to see what it was. McGinley was immediately distracted by the noise, and his task of getting up was completely forgotten. He went still as he tried to look toward the sound, listening for it to occur again. Everything was a bit foggy, as though there was some kind of film over his eyes, and this fact forced him to quiet himself.

Suddenly, something darted toward him, scrambling in his direction. It latched itself onto his arm, and he felt that irritating pressure once again. McGinley reached with his free hand and grabbed onto the object, and it immediately gave a piercing squeal. He tried to hold it up to his face to see it better, but it seemed to be attached to him somehow. He gave it a hard yank, and it came free, pulling a long scrap of flesh from his arm as it did so.

The CEO of Aspen Stationers' held the squirming thing before his face and tried to look around the milky fog in his eyes. It screamed and squirmed violently, putting up a heck of a fight. Right away McGinley could smell it; it smelled of metal and rot, but to him, it smelled like dinner, and Roger was overcome with ravenousness right away.

He put the creature directly into his mouth, disregarding all of its movement and struggle. With one demanding bite, he sunk his teeth into it, and hot blood flowed over his tongue, causing him to close his eyes with great satisfaction and pleasure. He chewed and chewed as the rat's bones crunched in his mouth like a handful of roasted peanuts.

Its body went limp in his hand, but he held onto it like a gory candy bar. He had taken off its head cleanly; the thing would come to life no more. The only thing Roger McGinley was aware of was the incredible flavor of the thing; he could care less about what it was or what he was doing to it.

For the next twenty minutes, he sat on the floor of the lab with flesh and blood-filled hand and ate the monstrosity of a rat which had become his snack. When it was finally gone, McGinley once again attempted to look around the room. In no time he resumed his struggle to rise from the floor; trying to figure out who, or what, he was.

Captain Hertz arrived at Aspen right around the time Roger McGinley finished eating his little meal. Randy attempted to fill him in on what was happening in the building, but it proved to be harder than he thought. Every man there thought the scientist had plumb lost his mind. They devoted more energy to rolling their eyes at each other than they did in trying to believe him.

Finally, with his frustration at its peak, Randy pulled his thumb drive from the front hip pocket of his trousers and began to wave it around.

"It's all right here, I'm telling you!" His voice was becoming extremely desperate. "I was in charge of this project, of the testing, of the ink! I'm telling you that it is doing something… something that I can't explain and Roger McGinley is in there!"

Hertz glanced over all the men standing in amused attention. Yes, he thought he was listening to the rantings of a madman, but something in his stomach was telling him that, even if it was all baloney, this guy believed everything he was saying, and maybe Hertz should be giving his words a bit more credence.

"Okay," he finally said. "I'm gonna take Gibbons in, and we're going to see what the heck is going on in there." He turned back to Randy. "Now I'm gonna tell you, if you're sending me in this place on some kind of prank or wild goose chase, I'm going to see to it that you sit in my jail for the longest amount of time possible under the law, got that?"

Randy immediately let out a sigh of relief and nodded. "Fine. If that's what you want. You're going to find out in a minute that I'm serious." His eyes went wide then. "You will need something… some kind of protection."

Hertz's face went stern, and his voice turned to steel. "I'm not gonna go all out for this, do you understand? If there is some kind of problem when I get in there I'll make my decisions accordingly from there, but for now, we will simply go in, guns drawn."

He turned back to Gibbons. "Ready?"

The man nodded, and together, with Teddy, they proceeded through the gate. Randy and the rest of the officers watched as they neared the building, and then finally went around to the back lab entrance. Randy turned to the men and crossed his arms over his chest.

"If I were you, I'd be preparing for a heck of a Sunday, guys."

CHAPTER 13

Both Hertz and Gibbons had chatted nervously on their way to the building. Even if Dr. Carstens was out of his mind, he was likely telling the truth about the rats attacking, and neither of them wanted to get bitten. In all truth, they only had their guns drawn to blow away the disgusting rodents, and that was all.

With Dr. Carstens' key, the door to the Aspen Stationers' lab entrance came open easily.

Captain Hertz and Officer Gibbons entered the narrow, institution-like hallway, guns drawn. There were doors on both sides, set into the large white cinder block walls. Some of them had long windows alongside them. According to Randy, the last place he had seen Roger McGinley had been in the lab, getting eaten by rats, and that would be the second door on their left after they entered. It would have the longest windows, all shaded.

They were about ten feet from the lab door. "It's open," Hertz said in a low voice. He stopped in his tracks and went still, trying to hear what he could. The sound of scuttling and shuffling came to both of their ears.

Hertz looked at Gibbons. The man looked confused as if he were trying to identify the sounds and couldn't place them. After a moment of nervousness, Hertz had had enough.

"This is Captain Eli Hertz," he shouted. "I'm with the Monte Vista police. Is anyone in there?"

There was no response, only more shuffling.

The two men inched toward the door, and Hertz continued. "Are you hurt? Do you need medical attention?"

Silence still. Right then Gibbons got a whiff of some kind of stench, and it made him gag slightly. Hertz turned to him and gave him an angry look before gesturing with his head for the man to advance.

Gibbons closed his eyes and took a breath, then went on. "Police!" he shouted loudly. "We are coming into the lab; if you have any weapons, put them down, and raise your hands above your head!"

He took one long stride then turned into the room, his gun out in front of him crazily. In the lab were cage after cage of unidentifiable animals. Gibbons' eyes grew as wide as saucers as he watched the blood-covered balls of fur race to and fro in their cages. On the floor was smeared blood, and a lot of it; in the middle of that was what appeared to be a patch of bloody fur.

Right then one of the creatures raced across the floor about five feet in front of him. He opened fire, hitting it right away. It flew against one of the cabinets, left a splatter of blood, and then it hit the ground. Bits and pieces of it surrounded its insane-looking body.

But there was no man in there at all.

Hertz was right by his side. "What in the heck is that?" He was referring to the animal Gibbons had shot.

"A rat?" Gibbons said with disbelief.

"It doesn't look like a rat to me," his captain replied. "And where the heck is this McGinley guy anyway? That must be his blood."

Gibbons began to step forward toward the cages. "Or the blood of something. Look at this, Captain! That guy wasn't kidding about these things!"

Hertz joined the officer, and together they began to walk from cage to cage. The rats inside were unrecognizable; all of them were missing at least one limb. Others were peering out of a single eye, or even feeling their way around blindly. One of the cages held three rats, and two of them had begun to tear away at another. Crunching sounds accompanied by screeching began to come from the cage, and Gibbons turned away and promptly threw up on the floor.

The captain ignored the man. He was in such shock at what he saw that he could do nothing but stare at the cages. When Gibbons was through he stood, hunched over with his hands on his knees, his pistol still in one hand, but only barely. Out of the corner of his eye, something moved, and he jerked, pulling his gun back up and to attention.

The rat, the one he had shot, began moving.

It was squirming in its own blood. There was a hole directly through the center of its body, ragged and charred, from the bullet. But it was moving, and it was trying to pull itself toward him on its two front legs, or what remained of them.

"Oh, no way," Gibbons stuttered, his free hand going up to cover his mouth as if to stop the next rush of vomit, along with the fear. "Captain Hertz…"

Hertz spun around and looked at Gibbons, then his eyes followed the officer. He took one look at the rat, which had made a bit of progress, and his mind almost snapped. Hertz's hands began to tremble violently.

"What in the heck?"

Now the thing started to move a bit faster, picking up its pace in an effort to reach Gibbons, almost as if it could smell his debate to run screaming or not. Hertz wasn't as frozen in place. Even with his hands shaking he double tapped his trigger. The first bullet missed. The second hit it in the rear sending it flying. It rocketed through the air, blood flying from its mangled body, and landed in the corner.

When it landed, Hertz's first thought was that what was once the rat's head was now gone.

He turned to Gibbons to see if the man was okay; frustrated that all the officer had done was puke almost since the moment they arrived. He needed the guy to get himself together, and the sooner the better. They needed to find the supposed victim, Roger McGinley.

"Listen, now's the time to…"

Hertz caught movement out of the corner of his eye. It was movement, slow and jerky, and it was right behind Gibbons, who had his back to the door, still doubled over and green at the gills. The captain spun all the way around, his focus on what he had first thought was a shadow. He realized with horror that he was sadly mistaken.

It was a man, or at least Hertz thought it was a man. His mind raced to find the right words to holler at the cop he had brought in as a partner, but what his eyes saw his mind could not wrap around. If it was a man, it was a mere shell of one.

There were holes in his face. His cheeks were nearly gone, any skin that did remain was ragged and torn. One eye hung lazily from its socket, almost staring at the floor as if to assist him in watching where he was walking. His neck was nearly non-existent, and Hertz could see his spine clearly through the gaping hole. He was missing fingers from both hands, and his clothes had been gnawed clear through in random spots. Blood seeped through everywhere and covered the flesh that did remain.

Captain Hertz took in all of it in only seconds, but the sight froze him in his place. This monster making its way into the room, nearly lunging to the sickly Gibbons, had to be Roger McGinley. It was horrifying and grotesque, a staggering pile of death which was sucking the blood from what remained of its own lips as its arms reached out for the cop in the middle of the room.

"Gibbons, look out!"

Hertz raised his gun once again and managed to fire a few shots, but then it was out of bullets. Gibbons jerked upward and around, a stringer of his regurgitated lunch hanging from his bottom lip, swinging upward and sticking to his own cheek. But even as Hertz fought to reload his weapon with trembling hands, he knew that Gibbons would not be able to get away.

He yelled piercingly just as the McGinley monster grabbed hold of Gibbons by his left arm. He tried to jerk away, but so solid was the grip he had on the cop that it stopped him dead in his tracks. A look of severe pain came over his face, causing him to close his eyes and his mouth to fly open wide. His scream turned into a whining gurgle, and he dropped to his knees.

McGinley dropped down next to him without missing a beat. When he tore his teeth into Gibbons' forearm, the man found his voice once again. The scream was deafening, and Hertz managed to drop the bullets which he was trying to put into his gun.

At last, the captain realized the true desperation of the situation. He grabbed his radio from his belt and began to yell into it: "Backup! I need backup in here now!"

Next, he dropped his radio to the ground and proceeded to try to load the gun once again, but he knew his attempt was going to be futile. He continued to glance up from his loading to see that McGinley, if indeed it was him, was now shaking his head violently back and forth, trying to rip Gibbons' skin from his arm. Droplets of blood were flying from the wound he was creating, but now the cop wasn't making a sound. Whether from terror or nausea, he passed out cold, a limp ragdoll in the hands of a bloodthirsty murderer.

As Hertz finally got the last bullet into the chamber,

he could hear the voices of some of his men coming, and relief washed over him as he aimed his gun. He shot the monster once in the chest and another time in the leg, but neither shot seemed to faze him in the slightest. He did nothing but jerk slightly, grunt with frustration, and continue to dine on Gibbons. Now he actually had the man's shirt up and was tearing into his stomach.

"Get off of him!" Hertz was starting to panic. He peeled off another two rounds, one hitting the creature in the arm and the other in his neck, but he just kept going.

Four officers came around the corner, along with Teddy and Randy Carstens. Bransky was leading the pack, and all of the officers had their guns drawn. At first they froze, stunned by what they were witnessing with McGinley and Gibbons. Bransky then seemed to snap out of it and take notice of Captain Hertz, who fired two more shots and was again trying to reload.

"Shoot it!" He screamed with both anger and fear.

Suddenly all of the firearms in the room seemed to go off at once. Teddy took off like a shot, being both sick to his stomach and filled with fear. Randy backed against the windowed wall, but he stayed, watching as McGinley's body was riddled with bullets, jerking like a puppet on so many strings. Randy took sharp notice of one thing, however: McGinley didn't 'die' until a bullet struck him in the head.

The monster fell face first to the floor, completely and realistically dead. All the men halted their fire and just stared, breathing heavily with wide eyes and gaping mouths. It was a scene to behold, Randy thought as he scanned each and every man in the room.

Suddenly Gibbons' bloody body began to squirm.

"See if he's all right!" Hertz yelled to no one in particular.

"No!"

This came from Randy, who had suddenly stepped forward with his hands in the air.

"I'm telling you, he is like McGinley now," he said harshly. "Like the rats! He is not Officer Gibbons anymore."

They all glanced at him in disbelief but tried to keep their eyes on their comrade. He began to grunt and smack his lips. Then he began to struggle to get to his feet, his torn-up arm reaching out in a swinging motion as he tried to get his hand on anyone he could reach.

"No," Hertz said hesitantly. "It's Gibbons, I tell you."

The man reached down to help his friend up, but as soon as Gibbons got hold of his hand, he tried to pull it into his mouth. Captain Hertz jerked away with all his might and reactively shot him in the chest, sending him flying backward about four feet. He almost immediately began to make his way to another man, Officer Bransky.

"The head!" Randy yelled. "Shoot him in the head; it's the only way!"

Multiple gunshots rang out, and the corpse that used to be Officer Gibbons fell to the ground next to McGinley, dead at last.

CHAPTER 14

Diana raced from the staff lounge to the elevator in near panic. She attempted to contact Aspen Stationers' Supply Company, only to find that there was no answer. After a bit of research, she learned that the company had been closed down and was under quarantine due to some kind of 'outbreak.' All she wanted to do was find Dr. Hilliard, tell him what she knew, and determine the next best step for all of them to take.

The elevator was jam-packed when she arrived, so she darted for the stairs. The fifth floor was going to be quite a workout, but the thought never even entered her mind. All she wanted to do was get to ICU and stat.

As soon as she opened the door to the fire stairs, panting and sweating, she was greeted by nothing but noise and chaos.

Nurses and doctors were running here and there. There was a nurse on the floor in one corner, surrounded by her co-workers. Her arm appeared to be bleeding profusely, and she looked pale and ill. At the nurses' station, one woman was on the phone begging for what sounded like police assistance, but it was obvious she was getting nowhere.

From the looks of it, the city of Thornton was in the beginning stages of a disaster.

Diana reached out and grabbed a male nurse who was running by her. "Where is Dr. Hilliard? What the heck is going on here?"

When the man turned to her, she saw nothing but madness in his eyes. He looked at her, but it was obvious he didn't see her or hear her at all. He quickly jerked his arm away from her and began running once more. Right then she saw the nurse at the station slam the phone down, and she sped over to the woman.

"What's happening, nurse? Where is Kyle Hilliard?"

The nurse's face was wet with tears, and she had a panicky look in her eyes. "He took the Casperson girl's sister to a safe room."

"What?" Diana asked. "What do you mean, a 'safe room'?"

"The sick Casperson girl… she attacked her mother," the woman stammered. "The mother undid her restraints, and the girl suddenly… attacked her! The older one, she came running out, and they were chasing her, both of them! He took her away to keep her safe!"

The woman broke down in sobs, but Diana paid her no mind. Everyone on the floor was out of their minds, and from what she had just learned she knew that she had no time to waste trying to comfort the hysterical nurse. She darted in the direction of the elevators once again, but just as she reached them the nurse in the corner went crazy, kicking and clawing. When Diana turned in the direction of the commotion she saw the woman had a bloody grip on another attendant with her teeth.

The elevator came open, and she rushed inside, followed immediately by three more nurses and a janitor, all of whom were trying to escape the madness on the fifth floor. It was right then she also saw Julie Yates, the nurse who had checked the Casperson girl in. She was loping toward the elevator, spit stringing from her mouth, her skin yellowed and papery. The flesh was ripped away from one side of her face, and she was emitting a grunting scream, unlike anything Diana had ever heard.

"No!" the janitor yelled. "Shut the door! Shut the door now!"

He reached out and began to punch the button to close the elevator door over and over. It began to finally close in slow motion, with Yates getting closer and closer. It finally closed just as the woman lurched for it, sealing at the very last second.

It seemed that everyone in the elevator began to sob in relief all at once. Diana was panting, and her heart was pounding violently against her rib cage. All heck had broken loose at Suburban Medical Center.

She suddenly reached out and hit the emergency stop button. The elevator gave a violent jolt before screeching to a stop. All of the passengers began to scream at Diana.

She calmly held up her hands. "If we are in here, we are safe! I need you all to calm down, now!"

She was forced to repeat her statements another

time before they all began to be still once more. "Listen: I know we have a major issue going on, and a terribly dangerous one at that." Diana made it a point to make eye contact with everyone on the elevator as she spoke. "I think I know what the problem is, what has caused this… this outbreak. But I must know if any of you know where Dr. Kyle Hilliard is. He took the older Casperson sister off the floor for her safety."

"I do!"

It was the janitor, a man with 'Reese' on his identification badge.

"I'm Harold, Doctor, Harold Reese" he replied. "When everything started to go crazy Dr. Hilliard came up to me and asked me where my work quarters were located. He asked me if there was a lock on my office, and when I told him 'yes' he left with the little girl in his arms."

"A little blond girl, right?"

"Yes," Harold said. "A little blond girl."

"Where did you tell them to go?"

He smiled slightly, but his eyes were still wild with fear. "Why, to my office, of course. It's in the basement, on the opposite side of the floor from the lab, where the boilers are. The entire maintenance area can be locked. It is where to go in case of a shooting or anything."

Diana took a deep breath and smiled back at him. She punched the button, and after a violent jerk the elevator started up once again. Diana pressed the 'B,' and they were off.

"That is where we are going, then," she said. "It will be the safest place for all of us. Is there a phone in your office, Harold?"

"Of course there is."

"Then it's decided," Diana concluded.

∞

The fifth-floor intensive care unit at Suburban Medical was in far worse shape than either Dr. Hilliard or Dr. Moss could comprehend.

For one thing, many more people had been bitten and attacked than just Michelle, Julie Yates, and the nurse in the corner. Something of a chain reaction had been set off as soon as Melanie's mother had set her free of her restraints, and now, each and every patient on the floor was looking an awful lot like the rats looked at Aspen, and if Randy had been present, he would have vouched for that fact.

Kyle Hilliard had, indeed, taken Megan to the maintenance area. He had put her in Harold's office, fished a can of soda out of his mini-refrigerator for the child, and then locked her safely inside. Next, he had called the hospital administrator from a corridor phone and told him what was happening. The entire hospital was being put on lockdown just when Diana was pressing the elevator button to the basement. The administrator then locked himself in his office and proceeded to call the police, who were telling him of the situations breaking out all over the state of Colorado.

It was nothing short of a catastrophe.

Now, Kyle was back in Harold's office with little Megan. She was curled up in the corner, covered with Kyle's doctor coat and sipping pop. He was sitting in Harold's chair trying to figure out what to do next. Where had Diana disappeared to? He could only assume that one of the monsters had managed to get its hands on her somehow, which told him they had spread even further than he initially believed.

Suddenly he could hear a key being inserted into the office door.

Kyle jumped up from where he sat and practically threw his body into a protective shield in front of Megan, who had begun to cringe immediately with fear. The knob turned, and the door opened, and Harold and Diana nearly tumbled into the door. They were followed by a small group of emotional nurses, patients, and other hospital staff.

Kyle nearly collapsed. "Diana, Finally! I've been looking for you! The fifth floor is completely out of control, and I have no idea what the heck could be going on in the rest of the facility!"

"It's on complete lockdown," she gasped as she made her way, in surprise, to Kyle and Megan. "I've only gotten bits and pieces. I've been to the fifth floor; what can you fill me in on?"

Kyle turned himself over, his motions slow and exhausted. As he pushed himself against the wall for support he began, "I was talking to a nurse at the desk on five. The alarm started to go off in Melanie

Casperson's room, signifying that her restraints had been compromised. Just as I prepared to run to the room, Megan here came out, and she wasn't moving too slowly. Michelle had loosened Melanie's restraints, and the girl had attacked her. Megan barely made it out. After that, everything went sort of haywire."

Diana sat cross-legged on the floor by both of them while Harold locked the office up tightly. He then picked up the receiver of the phone on his desk and began to punch out numbers while they continued to talk. She wanted to know everything she had missed during her trip to purchase the Lumiosa pen and while taking it to the lab.

"I got one of the pens at the pharmacy, just like you said," she told Megan. "When I got back here I took it to the lab to a man named Roy." She glanced at Kyle. "You know, Roy Fitch. He did some tests, and he said that the ink is likely the problem. It destroys all cells it comes into contact with while simultaneously… mutating them and keeping them alive, but they become volatile."

"Are you serious?" Kyle asked her.

Diana could do nothing but nod. She paused for a long moment, then continued. "I tried to contact Aspen to initiate a complaint for recall, but the entire factory has been shut down and quarantined, and there is some kind of… outbreak… in the town where the company is located: Monte Vista."

"So, what now?"

"Well," Diana said as she shot a brief look at Megan

then back to Kyle.

Wasting no time, Kyle rose to his feet and walked over to Harold, who was just hanging up the phone. "Was that administration?"

The older man looked at him with tired eyes and nodded his head.

"Well, what did they say?"

Without changing his expression at all the janitor said, "It was the administrator's secretary. The entire hospital is on red alert lockdown. Everyone is to stay where they are until they are notified otherwise, and if possible, we are to remain under lock and key."

"I can't believe this is happening!" Kyle felt as if he were losing his mind. He looked at Diana, but her eyes were empty of the answers. They were all tired, hungry, and scared. They all needed some time to think about the situation they were in.

"Well," he said, turning to Harold, "what do you think?"

Harold released a ragged breath and sat on top of a box marked Bleach. "I'm not sure what the heck to think, to be honest with you." He looked at Diana. "How about you?"

"I think we need to stay right where we are for now," she replied.

The room fell silent except for the sobs coming from a few of the nurses. Even Megan was doing better than they were. She sat in the corner, wide-eyed, clinging to her soda can with one hand and stroking Kyle's doctor coat with the other.

After a moment the young girl spoke up. "What about my mom?"

All eyes went to her immediately. Kyle's mouth opened slightly as if to respond, but he remained still, obviously at a bit of a loss for words. Instead, Diana, who had been the girl's pediatrician since birth, reached out and took Megan's free hand. As she stroked it with her thumb, she offered up a slight smile.

"She is upstairs, Megan, and she is pretty sick too, just like Melanie."

Megan nodded. She put the can on the floor and pulled the doctor coat over her head. It was a reply that everyone in the room understood clearly. One of the nurses broke out into a fresh batch of tears.

It looked like it was going to be a long stay for the group in the basement at Suburban Medical Center.

R.W.K. Clark

CHAPTER 15

It seemed to Randy that the police station was in a state of madness. He sat in a chair watching people rush to and fro like they were mad. People had been pouring in, attempting to get information on what had taken place at Aspen, and the phones were ringing off their hooks, but the police were trying to keep it tight-lipped. They didn't want to breed panic, but someone on the inside had obviously already run his mouth, and word of the horrible incident was spreading like wildfire.

The incident at Aspen Stationers' had managed to take the lives of both Roger McGinley and Officer Gibbons, but it was apparent that the situation was not confined to Monte Vista. Just since he had been sitting there, his smartphone had alerted him to another outbreak incident in the town of Thornton, and from the way it sounded, things were looking mighty bleak. People were actually holing up for safety in the local high school! Randy's blood was running cold, and his mind would not stop its thinking and wondering; how many people all over were actually being affected?

Randy knew that, as far as Monte Vista went, the only known infected beings were the rats, and they were caged up. All of them but the one cage that fell. He remembered that three of them attacked Roger McGinley, but only one was there when they re-entered the lab, and that one had eventually been shot to death. He had made the police aware of that fact, but it didn't make a difference. Aspen and all of the property that was part of the company were shut down immediately and quarantined until such a time as things could be figured out and the problem solved. Randy knew that wouldn't matter to an infected rat.

The doors to the station flew open once again, and a woman came in screaming. She was one of many who appeared to be panicking, or at least that was how it seemed initially. Randy stared at her; most of his view was obstructed by the massive desk which sat directly in front of the main entrance, so all he could see was her face. She was crying, and he could make out the words 'help me' when she spoke, but that was all.

He stood and made his way closer to the main desk.

"All I want is for someone to look at him," she was sobbing. "I just want to know if he is infected with this… this thing! I know something is going on; everybody knows!"

The officer at the desk was trying to calm her with soothing words, but she was having no part of it.

"Listen to me!" she continued, her eyes becoming wilder. "He was fine! He was just playing, and then that animal bit him, and it's like he passed right out! He's cold! Someone just look at him, please! He's out in the car!"

That managed to really get Randy's attention. He walked straight up to the desk and began to talk to her without even thinking about whether or not he should. He wanted to know the details right away.

"Excuse me, ma'am," he said as he touched her arm. "What bit him?"

She turned to him immediately, a look of relief coming over her face. "Finally, someone is going to listen! I don't know what it was. It came into our yard where my Timmy was playing; I saw it coming toward him up the sidewalk. I thought it was a small cat or something."

She took Randy by the arm and began to lead him to the main entrance. "Just look at him, please! The thing bit him, and he passed out almost right away, then it began to… to… try and eat him!"

Randy followed her, but he already knew; it was the rat he was just wondering about that had bitten this boy. Behind him he could hear the officer at the desk yelling at him to come back, an officer would handle it, but Randy ignored the man and went out the door with the woman.

She continued to talk as they walked, her words pouring out of her mouth at high speed. "I just ran outside and tried to shoo it off, but it tried to come at me. I picked up a large rock and smashed it! I smashed it and grabbed my boy and put him in the car."

They were nearing a blue car. At first, the car looked empty and peaceful. When they got about ten feet from it a small, blond-haired boy sat straight up and began to pound on the glass of the window. He had what looked to be red, bloody bite marks on his forearms and face, and his eyes were insane. He immediately began to scream and growl at them both.

"Timmy?" The woman jumped back, startled at first, then completely overcome with fear. "Timmy?"

Randy reached out and grabbed her by the upper arm, pulling her backward. "You can't go near it," he said. "Yes, he is sick. He has the sickness."

She looked at him with wide-eyed dismay. "No! How do you know?"

"Is the car locked?"

She nodded. "And the window lock is on, as well as the child safety locks."

"We have to keep him in there," he told her. "We need to get an officer right now."

He still had a firm grip on her arm. "I can't leave him! He needs me!"

She tried to put up a fight, but Randy wasn't about to let go of her. "You don't understand! He is not himself, and he will hurt you! Didn't you say you heard about the sick man at Aspen?"

"Yes, but…"

Randy stopped and looked her dead in the eye, his face stony and serious. "We have to get a cop, okay? I know it is your son. I have kids too;.but he is sick, and it is very dangerous, okay?"

After a second she nodded mutely, looking as if she were dazed and very confused. Randy began to walk back into the police station briskly, pulling her along behind him. She stumbled over her own feet as she tried to keep up.

Back in the station, there was still a small group of people around the main desk, all of them trying to talk to the officer seated there. In their efforts, each of their voices fought for power, and the result was nothing short of chaotic. Randy cut through the crowd, keeping a firm grip on the woman the entire time.

"Officer," he said, leaning down into the cop's face. "This woman, the one with the boy..." he turned to her briefly.

She understood immediately, and said, "Linda Abbott."

"This is Linda Abbott," Randy continued. "She is the one with the boy who got bit. He is in the car, and officer, he is very sick."

Randy was trying his best to keep his voice down but still audible, but that was much easier to do in theory. "What?" the cop asked as he turned his ear to Randy.

At that point, Randy's frustration was bordering on explosive. He grabbed the officer by the shoulders and practically pressed his lips against the guy's ear. "Her boy is very, very sick! He has been infected!"

The cop looked at him, all of the color draining from his face. He may not have been one of the cops on the scene at the Aspen Company, but word had already gotten around the entire department about Gibbons and the rats, and it came from the Captain himself. He believed his boss.

The man wasted no more time. Instead, he jumped up from his seat at the desk and grabbed another officer. "What vehicle is it?" he asked Randy as the four of them headed for the door.

"It's a blue car parked on the curb out front," he replied. "It is locked, and the child safety locks are engaged, his mother said."

Linda Abbott followed numbly behind them, and the group that had been at the desk began to follow as well. They got halfway down the main walk when the desk officer, whose chest tag read 'D. Mason', stopped and held up his hands. "Listen, folks, I'm going to have to ask you to return to the station. This is nothing more than a professional police matter and has nothing to do with your own inquiries. Please re-enter the building; another officer will be with you shortly."

The crowd began to mumble and complain, but they all started back for the building. Right then Randy saw three more cops coming from the side of the building, and they were headed in their direction. Officer Mason didn't take notice; he simply started for the blue car once more, the other cop close by his side.

"Nobody hurt him, please." Linda began to sob. "He is just a little... just a boy!"

Mason turned to her. "Ma'am, no one is going to get hurt if we can help it. I need you to go into the station with the others, please."

Linda looked up at Randy, who nodded at her. He intended to stay, but the cop soon said, "you too, sir."

"But I am the scientist who engineered this strain,"

he retorted. "I think it's important that you have someone with you who knows what is going on. Wouldn't you agree?"

Mason thought about it, then turned to the officers who had joined them. "Will one of you take this woman back inside please?"

One of the cops, a female, stepped forward and smiled at Linda Abbott before taking her gently by the arm and leading her away. "Please, please don't hurt him!" she kept saying as they walked away.

Now the group turned back in the direction of the car, which sat quietly on the curb, appearing to be empty. They were only about seven feet from the car, but even from that close proximity, it looked dead and empty. No one moved; they all simply stared at it.

"This is the vehicle, sir?" Dean Mason asked Randy.

"Yes, Officer. It…"

His response was immediately interrupted by the reappearance of the boy. So quickly had he popped up that everyone in the small group jumped back, one of them even shouting in fear. Timmy pressed his gray, torn face against the glass and started his hollering and grunting, and his tiny fists began to pound once again.

"What the heck…?" Mason was stunned, not only by the surprise appearance but by the way the boy looked. Even Randy thought that he looked worse than he had only minutes before.

His face was more than gray, it was sunken, and there was a pasty appearance to the flesh itself. The bite marks which were all over him were crusted with blood, and it resembled raw meat. His eyes showed the most change—his irises and pupils were almost completely covered in white.

"He's all the way gone, you guys," Randy said with disgust.

The child responded violently to their voices, becoming more and more combative as he attacked the inside of the car trying to get out and get to them.

"What is he trying to do?" Mason asked without looking away.

Randy just stared. "He is trying to get out so he can eat us."

Mason took his radio off his hip. "I'm going to need a backup team out in front of the station, and keep the public from leaving the building. We have a major situation out here."

"Ten-four," a bodiless voice replied.

Now he turned to Randy and the other cops. "Is there a way we can contain him without hurting him?"

"None, other than keeping him locked up tight," Randy replied.

Right then a group of officers, led by Captain Hertz, came out of the station house. Two of them stayed behind and guarded the doors to ensure that citizens didn't come out and endanger themselves. The captain and the others jogged over to the blue car.

"What do we have, Mason?" Hertz asked.

Mason cleared his throat. "A young boy, Timmy Abbott. His mother came in upset, saying that the child had been playing and was attacked by an animal she didn't recognize. It was biting him and trying to eat him. He passed out, and she came to the station to find out if his condition fit in with the Aspen situation."

Hertz's eyes were glued to the boy in the car window, he looked to be getting a bit ill by what he saw. Now the child turned to the back of the seat and began ripping and tearing at the upholstery, and he seemed to be doing it with ease. It seemed to Randy that the grown men stood there forever just staring, and he found himself wondering if anyone at all was trying to figure out their next step.

Finally, Hertz spoke up. "We need to get him out of that car and into a tightly confined space. We have to figure this damn mess out." Now he turned to Randy. "Police and city officials in Thornton have a serious outbreak of the same going on right now."

Next, he turned to the officers who had come out with him. "Randall, go into storage and get that bite suit from the K9 program, double time."

The man took off like a shot, leaving Hertz to continue. "This is what we are going to do: I'm going to have Randall put on the bite suit since he was trained in the old K9 program; his experience with dogs should help us out here. Mason, I want you to call Monte Vista Medical Center and get Dr. Jarvi, the psychiatrist, on the phone. We need some professionals and some proper restraining gear to get this boy to a place where all of us are safe.

"The last thing I want is to have to take the boy's life. I'm going in to see the Mayor about putting in calls to the Feds. Get moving." He motioned to the last two officers standing there. "You two stay here. We'll all be back shortly. Keep people away from the scene."

Everyone seemed to take off at once except for Randy and the last two cops. He looked at them, somewhat sheepishly. "Do you think maybe I should leave?"

They glanced at each other. "Weren't you involved down at Aspen?"

Randy nodded.

The cop shook his head. "No. You should probably stay. If the captain wants you gone, he can tell you himself."

With that, the officers proceeded to begin to direct pedestrians away from the vehicle. Randy stood, frozen in place, staring at the child in the blue car. It all felt like a very bad dream.

But he couldn't wake up; at least, not yet.

∞

Captain Hertz and a handful of officers surrounded the blue car outside of the police station. An officer in a bite suit stood closest to the vehicle, while all the rest of the men had their weapons trained on the small boy inside. The boy was thrashing about wildly, clawing at the window, and screaming at the top of his lungs. Randy had moved just inside the doorway to the station, where he stood with Linda Abbott, the boy's distraught mother. Her hand was over her mouth, tears were running down her face, and her shoulders were heaving with the force of holding back her sobs.

From the door, Randy could see the officers conferring. Another group of cops holding back the public and their prying eyes. It was all a very grim situation, and Randy knew full well the potential for disaster which loomed outside. He closed his eyes and silently prayed; he didn't even believe that the situation would turn out all right.

"Mason, go in and get the keys from Mrs. Abbott. She should be just inside the station," Hertz said in a low voice to his crew. Mason bolted for the building while he continued. "Okay, here it is: I'm going to unlock the vehicle with the remote if it has one. If not, I'll use the key." He turned his full attention to the officer in the bite suit. "Randall, when I get the door unlocked the rest of us are going to stand back, guns drawn, and you are going to get inside and grab him. There's the ambulance now; they'll have the restraint jacket I've requested, as well as a sedative."

The ambulance pulled up askew with its back end to the car; police got on either side of it to continue controlling the crowd. Two emergency medical techs got out of the rear of the vehicle; one carried a small, dirty straitjacket, and the other had a metal box, which the captain assumed held the medication and syringe they would need.

"Captain Hertz?" The first EMT approached the captain with the straitjacket in tow. His partner stood behind him, his eyes glued to the boy in the car, who was now beginning to foam at the mouth. "We're here to assist in the situation as you requested. What would you like us to do?"

Hertz gave the two men a brief rundown of the plan he had made upon their arrival. When he was finished, he looked at the second EMT. "Are you going to be administering the sedative?"

The young man nodded nervously, his eyes still on the boy, who was now beginning to bang his head on the window. A large chunk of gray flesh tore away from his forehead and stuck to the glass, but the child continued to bang away. The EMT's hands were trembling so badly that the box in his hands was rattling slightly.

Hertz watched the man, doubt beginning to build in his mind. "Excuse me," he said. "What is your name?"

The frightened young man didn't even flinch. Hertz turned to the first one, who responded to the question right away. "I'm Williams; this is Dowd." He reached out and grabbed his partner by the arm. "Dowd, we need you to pull yourself together!"

Dowd snapped out of it, jerking his head toward his partner, then to the captain. "S-S-Sorry, sir. What do I need to do?"

"Well, you were going to be administering the sedative as soon as Officer Randall there had the child subdued, but it looks to me as if you aren't the man for the job at all."

That statement seemed to get Dowd's attention, and he straightened his shoulders right away. After clearing his throat, he claimed. "No, sir. Not at all. I'm ready and capable."

With that, he set the metal box on top of a concrete half-column and prepared the sedative in the syringe. Once that was complete he turned back to the men. "I'm ready."

"Okay, then," Hertz said with a sigh just as Mason appeared with Linda Abbott's keys. He handed the captain a loud rhinestone-covered keychain in the shape of an 'L' with five keys on it.

"No remote, sir," Mason told him. "But the ignition key works all locks as well."

Hertz took the keys. "All right, Williams. I will be unlocking the passenger-side front door. All of my men will be standing behind us, but I will need you directly behind myself and Randall, and you will need to be ready with the injection and jacket. Dowd, as soon as Randall has him down and secured, you will administer the shot. We wait for it to take effect, and once that is done, Williams will put the jacket on the boy and you two will transport him to the psych unit. Everyone got it?"

The word "sir" echoed through the crowd of officers as everyone took their places, aiming their weapons as they settled in.

"Don't hurt him!" Linda Abbott was hollering from the front of the station. "Oh, please don't hurt my son!"

Hertz took hold of his radio. "I need an officer to keep Ms. Abbott in the building, please."

In seconds, Linda Abbott was taken back into the station. Captain Hertz looked around at the men, who all stood with a cross between expectation and petrifying fear on their faces. When he spoke, the captain's voice was filled with both compassion and determination.

"We have to do this men," he began. "Now, the most important thing is to be on your toes with the boy at all times. It may cost you your life to slack from paying attention for even a fraction of a second."

With that, Captain Hertz stood back and held up both hands to his team. "On three, Randall. One… two… three!"

Hertz put the key into the keyhole. In what seemed like slow motion he turned it with his right hand, and with his left hand flipped the door handle. He maintained both patience and self-control as he continued to hold the door shut, all while slowly letting it out a fraction of an inch at a time.

Officer Randall, sporting the bite suit, was positioned to Hertz's left, where he stood at the door's opening. In the seconds that Hertz was unlocking and opening the door, little Timmy Abbott was continuing to claw at the window while focusing his eyes on what the two men were doing. His face even changed as he realized that the men were, going to open the car door.

Timmy didn't change position until the door was ajar about six inches. It was then, suddenly and with great force, that the child seemed to scale the front passenger seat and throw all of his weight against the passenger door. So quickly did it happen, in fact, that both Hertz and Randall were instantly startled, and that enough to jump back about a foot apiece.

Which was all little Timmy Abbott needed.

Randall was waiting, arms extended, when the child hit the door which Captain Hertz was opening. The captain was taken off guard as the door hit him, knocking him backward onto his rear end. He emitted a loud 'ooooff!' when falling onto his back, knocking his head on the concrete.

Officer Randall was stunned by the boy's sudden movement as well, but quickly regained his wits and shot forward in an effort to grab the kid up and into his arms. He wrapped them around the child tightly, but the boy was much stronger than he looked, and Randall had not expected his strength at all. His arms and legs began to fly all around as he fought the man and the embrace, and he sank his teeth into the bite suit, shaking his head back and forth as a dog or wolf would do to its prey.

Now it was Dowd's turn to act, and it seemed that everyone turned their eyes to him all at once in anticipation of his move. Dowd just stood there, frozen in his place. His right hand gripped the syringe, holding it needle-up. His eyes were wide, and his mouth was wide open, but he didn't even flinch.

"Dowd!" Captain Hertz was sitting up, rubbing his head and struggling to stand. "Dowd, give him the shot!"

The man's lips began to move as if he was trying to say something in response, but no sound came out. Hertz finally got to his feet and limped his way as quickly as he could to the catatonic EMT. "Dowd!" He screamed directly in the man's face, but once again, the man didn't even flinch.

Hertz turned to see that Randall, who was still struggling violently with the infected boy, was on the losing end of the fight. Now he had the kid by only one arm, and the child was going completely haywire, squirming and twisting and biting at anything that came close to his mouth. Randall was about to lose control of Timmy Abbott, and he knew it full well.

"I need help!" he hollered just as Hertz turned back to Dowd and grabbed the syringe from his hands. The captain ran over to Randall, who was still clinging to the boy's arm with all his strength.

With a swing of his arm, Hertz stabbed the kid with the needle, and as soon as it was in, he drove the plunger home. Timmy jerked violently when it was administered, causing the captain to lose his own grip on the needle. The man staggered backward, his breath coming in pants and gasps. Timmy gave yet another jerk, twisting his body at the same time, and suddenly he broke free of Randall's hold altogether.

The boy stopped and looked around at the crowd. Everyone stepped back in fear as his eyes fell on each and every one of them. He seemed to be trying to get a grasp on his new-found freedom, though it had only been seconds since he gained it. As he opened his mouth and let out a vile, gravelly scream, and a piece of flesh fell from his forehead. Timmy took a step toward the captain.

"I don't think the shot is going to work," EMT Williams said in a low voice.

Timmy turned to him and suddenly charged at the man. Williams dropped the straitjacket he was holding and broke into a run. Hertz didn't miss a beat; he grabbed up the jacket and darted after Timmy, who was lurching after Williams. Hertz suddenly tripped over his own feet and fell hard to the ground.

Suddenly, shots seemed to ring out in every direction.

As the bullets hit the boy, his body jerked, making him look like a macabre marionette. None of the shots took him down, and he continued forward, unfazed and seemingly very determined. A scream came from the entrance area of the police station, and Linda Abbott suddenly appeared, running for her son and screaming hysterically.

"Don't shoot!" She yelled at the top of her lungs. "Don't hurt him!"

She was closing the gap between her and her son while all of the officers held their guns, frozen, in a position to fire once again. When Linda Abbott was about five yards from Timmy, he turned to her, just taking notice of her presence. In only fractions of a second, she reached the boy, and with one deft move scooped him up into her arms in an effort to protect him from further gunfire.

But Timmy was no longer Timmy, and he had other things on his mind.

She hadn't even come to a stop when he sank his teeth into her shoulder through her blouse. Now Linda was screaming, but it was no longer to stop the police from firing. Now her screams were filled with pain, and shock was all over her face as her mind tried to wrap itself around the fact that her son was biting her.

He began to shake his head violently back and forth as he tried to rip a bite of her flesh from her body. Blood was seeping through the cream-colored blouse in a pattern that resembled a blooming flower. Linda dropped to her knees and continued to scream.

Suddenly another shot rang out, and this one hit little Timmy Abbott directly in the side of his head. The entrance wound was small, but as the bullet exited it took a major amount of the child's brain with it. Tissue and bone fragments flew, and the boy went limp. His mother, who had been trying to pull him off of her, dropped him immediately to the ground, which he hit like a sandbag.

Linda was in shock. She sat on the ground, sobbing. Her hand went right to her shoulder and came away blood-soaked, causing her eyes to grow as wide as saucers. She looked up at Captain Hertz, her lips trembling, and disbelief all over her ghostly-white face.

"I tried to tell you, Ms. Abbott," he said with regret. "I tried to tell you to stay inside."

Her hands were trembling violently. She looked from them to the group of people standing around staring at her. Suddenly, her eyes rolled back into her head, and she began to convulse horribly. Gasps and muttered voices echoed throughout the crowd as the woman flopped around on the ground.

Williams, the EMT who still had his wits about him,

darted over to the seizing woman and knelt beside her. He began to administer medical attention, but Captain Hertz wanted him off of her right away. Didn't anyone understand anything?

"Williams, I need you to back away from Ms. Abbott," he said sternly.

The EMT turned to the man, a crazy look on his face. "There is no way I can ignore her need, sir."

"I'm not going to argue with you," the captain reiterated. "I need you to stand up and back away from her, right now."

The man glanced down at Linda Abbott. She had stopped seizing and was now lying peacefully on the ground. Her chest rose and fell with each breath she took, and he noted that her breathing appeared normal. Her skin had a grayish hue to it, though, and Williams was concerned about that.

"I need to treat the bite wound, Captain," he insisted. "She is continuing to lose blood."

Hertz shook his head. "Williams, she is now just like her son, and she will turn on all of us. I need you to step away from her immediately."

The look on the EMT's face changed as if he suddenly gained the understanding of what the captain was talking about. He slowly began to stand, using his hands to push himself up off the ground. As he rose, he turned to Hertz.

"Okay, sir. I'm going to…"

Linda Abbott's eyes flew open, and she had a hold of his arm in mere seconds; she had her teeth buried in his wrist in the blink of an eye.

Once again, gunfire rang out from all around, but this time most of the bullets fired hit the woman directly in the head, blowing it apart like a melon. It seemed that most of the officers had gained a clear understanding of the fact that only a headshot was going to stop the monsters they were dealing with. Even as her body lay lifeless, though, they all stood, guns drawn, ready to pump her full of lead once again if they had to. Soon EMT Williams turned as well.

What was happening was finally beginning to sink in.

The small town of Monte Vista was in for the nightmare of its life…

CHAPTER 16

The town of Monte Vista, Colorado was on the verge of making history.

By the time the upcoming school year was set to begin, the only people who could be found in the school were the residents of Monte Vista who had barricaded themselves in to save their own lives, adults and children alike.

Fortunately, calls were made, and by six in the morning that same day, the news was able to make an emergency alert regarding the state of the small town, which was far from good, and rapidly getting worse.

∞

"Good morning to those of you able to tune in today. It's Monday, August 17, and it looks like it will be a beautiful day weather-wise, but we will get to that in a bit...

"I'm Kelly Radcliffe, and this is the Channel Four News.

"State officials have received countless telephone calls from residents of Monte Vista, most of them starting last evening around five o'clock. According to the calls, there are individuals literally wandering the streets of the quaint town, violently attacking other residents, and in some reports even eating them. Monte Vista Mayor Tom Donnelly has currently called a 'state of emergency' for the town. Authorities are recommending that you do not, and I repeat, do not leave your homes for any reason. Keep all doors and windows locked, and remember to pull the shades and stay away from all windows.

"If for any reason you are not at home, and do not believe you can get to your home safely, emergency shelter is being offered at the Monte Vista High School. Police ask that you go directly there, and please, stop to talk to no one, and try to assist no one who appears to be in trouble.

"Dustin…"

The male anchor took over. "Good morning. I'm Dustin Goldman. At the current time, Federal authorities from the FBI to the Centers for Disease Control have dispatched teams to Monte Vista to investigate and subdue the situation there. Once again, remain in your homes or get to the high school; do not intervene in any attacks you may witness. Attackers appear to be infected with an unknown virus of some kind which has resulted in their violent state, and levels of infectiousness are unknown at this time.

"Stay tuned to Channel Four News for constant updates as to the state of the situation in Monte Vista…"

∞

Mayor Tom Donnelly aimed his remote control at

the flat screen hanging on his office wall and pressed the mute button, turning off the sound. He began to toy with the handheld device then, fidgeting with the buttons while the other men in his office waited in silence for him to speak. He shook his head in shock before opening his mouth.

"What the heck is going on here?"

He was making more of a statement than asking a question, and the others knew it. To his left sat the Monte Vista police captain Hertz, who was there to meet with the men after what he had experienced at Aspen, and next to him sat Rio Grande County Sheriff Burt Stahling. On his right was his trusted advisor Nicholas Stone, and beside him was city manager Clyde Smith.

All of the men were in a state of shock and confusion.

They waited for the phone to ring. Mayor Donnelly was expecting to hear from someone from the FBI to let them know they had arrived in town. He wanted them here, no, needed them here, yesterday. He was beside himself with concern and felt completely helpless being barricaded in City Hall like some chicken. He had been in a war, for sakes!

"Clyde, let's take it from the top again," he said flatly. "I want to know precisely where we are when these people arrive."

Clyde cleared his throat and grabbed a few sheets of paper from the edge of Donnelly's desk. "Chief Hertz's emergency dispatch received a call from one Doris

Fisher, sister of Maxwell, yesterday evening. She stated that her brother had gone to check on his neighbor, Paige Daugherty, and he didn't return for a significant amount of time."

He shuffled through the papers briefly, then continued.

"His slowness prompted Ms. Fisher to go check on him because they had dinner reservations," he said. "According to her, when she approached Daugherty's residence she observed one Kathy Olson and her son Brian leaving through the front door. They appeared to be severely intoxicated, and when they took notice of her, they turned in her direction and began to chase her."

Donnelly held his hand up to Clyde Smith, signifying he wanted him to briefly halt. He thought for a moment in silence, then motioned for the man to continue. Clyde cleared his throat once again.

"Doris Fisher said they were chasing her slowly, staggering. Almost struggling to walk. They only grunted; they didn't yell her name or anything. She claimed to be terrified that they were going to beat her up or something, though there was no reason, so she ran back to her brother's place. A ladder was against the side of the house, so she climbed it and pulled it up after her to keep them from going up. At that point she saw her brother and Ms. Daugherty approaching, staggering in the same manner.

"She also said each one of them was beaten, bloody, and torn up on their skin."

Donnelly stood up and grabbed a stress ball off his desk. He began to pace and toss the object from hand to hand. "What the heck does any of this mean?"

No one answered him. After a bit, Clyde cleared his throat once again to let him know he was going to keep going. The mayor understood, and Clyde, though terribly frightened and emotionally drained, did not object.

"Ms. Fisher also claimed that while she was on the roof of the home, the four individuals clawed at the house, and yelled unintelligibly at her. She stated that they growled and groaned more than anything else, making absolutely no sense. Another neighbor from across the street, one Marvin Potter, came running for them all in an attempt to offer Ms. Fisher assistance."

With this Clyde Smith stopped and took a deep breath. Even though he had read the report around seven times already during the meeting, it bothered him immensely to read the next part. He couldn't comprehend it, and frankly, he had a difficult time believing it to be true, even though he knew it was.

Once more, Clyde breathed out raggedly, cleared his throat as per his habit, took a deep breath, and began once more.

"Doris Fisher then says that the four on the ground turned on Mr. Potter in a manner that reminded her 'of a pack of dogs.' They ripped and tore at him, fighting with each other over him, and then began... eating him."

Clyde dropped the papers on the table with a bit of

dramatic flair, sat back in his chair, and began to rub his eyes. "I really don't want to have to read that again, Tom."

"Reading that is just the beginning, Clyde," Sheriff Burt Stahling said in a quiet voice. "It has quickly gotten much worse."

Mayor Donnelly stopped at the window to his office and crossed his arms over his chest. He continued to turn the stress ball around in his left hand as he gazed outside. He could see people running about, and he also had a clear view of two of the 'Deadwalkers,' as his own mind had started to call them. They were chasing what appeared to be a couple of teenagers.

The men fell silent once again, all of their eyes on the back of Mayor Donnelly, who was still looking out the window of his office at the violence and carnage taking place below. He had never seen anything like it; his town was literally eating itself alive!

How the heck would anyone, even the FBI or CDC, deal with this insane situation?

At that exact moment, the phone on his desk rang, emitting three consecutive chirps before briefly going silent and then repeating the pattern.

Donnelly crossed his office in two strides and plucked the telephone receiver from the base.

"This is Donnelly," he said in a deep, disturbed voice.

"Mayor Thomas Donnelly?" the voice on the other end inquired. "My name is Calvin Clemons; I'm an emergency response specialist for the Centers for

Disease Control with the United States government. We have just arrived in Monte Vista in response to a request for assistance with an unknown health threat."

Donnelly closed his eyes and breathed a massive sigh of relief. "Yes, Mr. Clemons. I'm so glad to hear from you. I called for assistance from both you and the FBI."

"Currently we are at the San Luis Valley Regional Airport," the man continued. "We have a team ready to go to work, along with agents from the FBI. Can you please give me a little more information on what is actually happening in Monte Vista?"

Donnelly's right hand went to his eyes and began to rub. "I don't know much. Yesterday one of our locals reported being nearly attacked by neighbors, who then proceeded to attack another neighbor and… eat him, right before her eyes."

"She knew the attackers?" Clemons asked.

Donnelly chuckled. "She not only knew them, but one of them was her brother."

Clemons did not respond right away to the words he heard. Donnelly waited, somewhat impatiently, even rolling his eyes as he kept his ears peeled for any sound from the other end. What the heck was going on with these people?

Finally, the man spoke. "Mayor Donnelly, we will need a safe base for operations. Where do you suggest we proceed to?"

"We have an emergency shelter set up at the high school. The only people you should find there are those who didn't make it home in time to be safe from the… Deadwalkers."

"Deadwalkers?" Clemons asked. "Did you just call them 'Deadwalkers'?"

Donnelly closed his eyes again, and a condescending smile came over his face. "Yes, I did. Why?"

"Why are you referring to them as 'Deadwalkers,' Mayor?"

He chuckled again. "Because they are dead, that's why."

The man on the other end of the line went silent. Donnelly waited patiently for him to gather himself; he knew what he had just said was particularly hard to digest. It was like something out of a nightmare or a bad movie.

Finally, Clemons spoke. "So, you are reporting that dead people are walking around, eating other people, and making more of the same? Do I have this right?"

Hearing the incredulity in the man's voice, the mayor began to get irritated. "Listen, my town is in a literal state of emergency. I don't care what it is that's causing this. I just want it stopped, and you people are the ones to call. So, you're here. What are you going to do?"

"Well," Clemons replied. "We are going to need transportation from here to the high school, and from there we will determine the next step."

When Donnelly finally hung up, he looked around at the other men in his office, all of whom were staring at him with expectant looks on their faces. After a moment his eyes settled on Sheriff Stahling.

"Burt, their team needs transportation to the high school from the airport," he said. "Please send three of your cars." He turned to Captain Hertz. "Could you do the same as well, Eli?"

The men both nodded and got on their cell phones immediately. Mayor Donnelly walked around to the chair at his desk and sat down hard. After rubbing his eyes, he shook his head.

"I don't know what these men are going to be able to do, but I sure as heck hope they do something fast."

R.W.K. Clark

CHAPTER 17

Agent Charles Cole of the FBI sat in the mayor's office at Monte Vista City Hall with another of his men, who sat next to him taking notes. Mayor Donnelly stared at him somberly as he spoke, with his own advisor, Nick Stone, busily taking notes as well.

"Mayor, the situation here in Monte Vista is, unfortunately, only the tip of the iceberg," he was saying in a monotone voice. "We have also had identical reports from around Colorado; Utah, Wyoming, New Mexico, and Kansas are also in the throes of this crisis, and teams have been sent there from the CDC, as well."

"What do they say is going on?" Donnelly asked as he leaned forward on his elbows.

Agent Cole avoided the mayor's eyes. "To be honest, we really have no idea. Not yet, anyway."

Donnelly stood up. "Come over here, Agent," he said as he walked to the office window.

Cole glanced at the other two men before standing and following the mayor.

"Look down there," Donnelly began. He pointed with his forefinger to the ground below, gesturing toward the violence and chaos going on beneath them.

"We are locked up tight in this building. Those that are here right now will not be allowed to leave until this issue is solved, and that includes you and your 'yes man' there. Is this really a situation you want to be stuck in?"

Cole watched the carnage. "Of course not, Mayor. I can tell you that the Army and National Guard are on the case, and they have discovered that destruction of the head is the only thing that will permanently disable these… 'Deadwalkers.' The CDC teams in all affected areas have several of them… disabled, and they are studying them furiously as we speak. That is all I can say."

Cole's partner spoke up. "We are safe here. Something is being done. But the infection process cannot truly be stopped altogether until we discover the source of it.

Charles Cole's cell phone began to chirp in his pocket. The silence of all the men in the office made the chirping seem extraordinarily loud. So loud, in fact, that Cole jerked, startled by the stark noise.

"This is Cole," he stated in a monotone voice into the phone.

He had the attention of everyone in the room. All of them stared, eager and expectant. At this point in the game, the caller could only be a handful of people: the CDC, other FBI, or someone much higher up on the political ladder. Whoever it was, all of them were anxious to hear from someone who could approve them to begin moving things along at a much faster rate.

A small, tinny mumbling was audible from the

phone, though the words that were being spoken could not be made out at all. Every now and then Cole would nod and say, 'mm-hmm.' Mostly, though, he simply stated 'yes sir' to most everything that was said to him.

Whoever was on the phone continued to speak for several minutes, and toward the very end of the call Cole closed his eyes and put his head in his free hand. It was a very hopeless gesture to all those in the office, and they all exchanged glances of doubt. Finally, Charles Cole flipped the cell shut, took a deep breath, and began.

"That was Calvin Clemons with the CDC team down at the high school," he said as he rubbed his forehead. "He had some good things to say, and some pretty scary things, as well. Heck, I'm not even sure where to begin."

"How about at the beginning?" Tom Donnelly asked with both sarcasm and frustration.

Cole shot him a look, took a deep breath, and began. "Well, it seems that the good news is this: one of the 'disabled' people who were infected was brought to Clemons with several others," he said, and then cleared his throat and sat back. "He began a general vivisection. On this particular individual, who happened to be an elementary-aged child. There were scrapes on his elbows, as if he had fallen on a sidewalk, or wrecked his bicycle. Around the scrapes on the child's right elbow was smeared ink, and according to Clemons it wasn't our typical ink."

"What do you mean?" Nick Stone asked with a knit

brow.

"Well, it seems that the ink was somewhat... three-dimensional," Cole replied. "As a matter of fact, Clemons says it was almost holographic in appearance, even on the child's skin."

Now Cole stood and began to pace as he talked. "So it now seems infected rats are not the only source. He did a bit of research, and he stated that it wasn't difficult to find out what it was: it was ink from a pen just released before the school year. The pen is called the Aspen 'Lumiosa,' and it is manufactured in a plant on the outskirts of town. A recall has been ordered, and I am to call the plant to demand the order be carried out as soon as I am finished. It seems, after testing, that the ink breaks down living cells and, according to Clemons' tests, also acts to keep the dead cells... animated."

"I don't understand," Donnelly said.

Cole turned to him. "It kills, but it keeps the things it kills alive. There is no other way to put it. Now, I have to contact the Aspen Company. If you gentlemen will excuse me for just a moment... Donnelly, may I use your computer to get some phone numbers, please?"

"Absolutely." The mayor went to his desk and signed himself into the computer, then moved aside so Cole could sit comfortably and do what he needed to do. No one said anything as he searched the Internet; the fact was, no one had anything to say.

After less than two minutes Cole picked up the phone on the desk and began punching in numbers. He put the receiver up to his ear and waited for a bit as the phone rang. It seemed to take forever for him to get an answer.

"Yes, this is Agent Charles Cole with the Federal Bureau of Investigation," he said. "To whom am I speaking?" After a moment of silence, he continued. "Mr. Jaynes, I need to speak with either the president or CEO of the company; it is a national emergency. Could you put me through please?"

He was silent again for a second, then said, "What exactly took place?"

This time he was still for a much longer period, and all of the color drained from his face as he listened to whatever the man on the other end of the phone was saying. At last he said, "Yes, I am aware of the incident. I will need you to give me the phone number of someone in charge, and I really don't care who. Their cell is preferred, and I would like their home phone as well, but I need at least one."

Cole took a pencil from the holder on Donnelly's desk and began to jot on the blotter which sat there as well. "Thank you for your assistance," he finally said, then he pressed the button to hang up, let up on it, and began punching numbers once again.

"Is this Thaddeus Greer of Aspen Stationers' Supply Company?" he asked.

After getting a response, he went through the tedious spiel of introducing himself before getting right to the point. "We have something of an epidemic spanning several states as a result of the ink you have used in your Lumiosa pen, and you will need to issue an immediate recall for the item. Before you ask, this is government-sanctioned, and if you give me your email, we will have an order sent to you immediately."

He listened for a moment longer, then added, "It will also need to be announced nationwide to the media; that is a priority. I will contact the three major networks; you contact your local channels right away. In light of what I learned happened to your president Roger McGinley, it is dire that we tend to this issue right away, with no procrastination whatsoever. Do you understand, Mr. Greer?"

At last, Cole hung up the phone, then turned his attention back to the computer.

∞

During Charles Cole's conversation with Thaddeus Greer, Captain Hertz of the Monte Vista police was telling all his officers to shoot them in the head, and it was directly afterward that his secretary came running from the building. "Captain," she began, "There is a call for you from a man named Cole from the FBI."

Hertz gave a few directives to his men, then followed her into the building to take the call. While they ran, she said, "You should also see the report on the news."

"Why?" he asked. "Is it about this situation?"

"Yes, and I think you are going to want to check it out as soon as possible."

Hertz made a beeline for his office and picked up the line Agent Cole was waiting on. "This is Captain Hertz," he said into the phone.

"Captain, my name is Agent Charles Cole, from the FBI," the man said, his tone all business. "I'm calling in reference to the quarantine that was ordered at the Aspen Company. You ordered that, am I correct?"

"Finally. Yes, I did," the captain replied. He then went on to try to fill Cole in on the unbelievable situation as best as he could. Even as he spoke, he thought it sounded ridiculous, but he pressed on.

When he was finished, Cole said, "You should know that similar reports are coming from a wide variety of locations in the United States. We are in a State of emergency. The good news is that we have narrowed down the issue to a specific type of ink that Aspen recently released."

"The Lumiosa pen," the captain said flatly as he reached up to rub his eyes.

There was a brief pause. "I take it you already knew this?"

"Well, to be honest," the captain replied, "Until the last hour I didn't realize the direness of the situation. We have a scientist from Aspen who developed the ink. He was the one who first called us to report an issue."

"I'm going to need to talk to him right away," Cole stated firmly. "As for now, you may have seen the news. At any rate, you will need to enforce a total lockdown. We don't have any idea how many may be infected, and it won't do to be lax about it until we know we have the issue under control."

Hertz thought briefly. "I'll contact our three local stations and put out an announcement. It will likely be far more effective if I set up a press conference. Obviously, we want the people to take action immediately."

Cole agreed, then gave the captain his cell number, reminding him to have Randy Carstens contact him right away. "From the sounds of it, we have much worse issues than you do at the current time, but we will stay in constant touch with you to keep you abreast of the situation as we go. I look forward to speaking with Dr. Carstens."

With that, the two men ended the call. Hertz had to sit down. The room was spinning, his head was aching, and he thought he might pass out from stress. He wasn't even sure what to do first, but finally he decided.

He picked up his phone and got in touch with his secretary. He told her to have Dr. Carstens come to his office right away. She quickly spotted the man and let the captain know he would be right in. Next, he began calling the networks and telling them they needed to have an emergency press conference, and he strongly reiterated how it couldn't wait. All three of them agreed to be at the station within the half-hour.

As Hertz hung up the phone, there came a light knocking on his office door.

"Yes?" he called out.

The door opened, and Randy entered. "Your secretary said you needed to see me right away."

The captain related to Randy everything that Agent Cole had told him. Next, he dialed the number to Cole and gave the receiver to the scientist, letting him know he was holding a press conference, and asking that he remain at the station for the time being. He then left the man alone to speak with Cole in private.

As promised, the news stations arrived in a very timely fashion. They had their equipment set up, ready and waiting for the announcement Captain Hertz was going to be making. As he made his way to the podium in the meeting room, Hertz took note of the fear on everyone's faces.

Yes, this was going to be one heck of a press conference, all right.

CHAPTER 18

Doctors Moss and Hilliard sat in the basement office of janitor Harold Reese in silence. So did everyone else in their company, including an exhausted and scared Megan. All of them had their ears peeled as they listened to the sounds which had started coming through the door only ten minutes before. Kyle turned suddenly to Harold. "Do you have any kind of radio in here at all?"

Nearly all of them had some type of smartphone, but the reception in the hospital basement was nonexistent. After taking turns trying, Harold pulled out the bottom file drawer on his desk. He pulled out a small pint of blackberry brandy, three thick manila envelopes, and finally a small transistor radio that had to be forty years old. Folded on top of it was a thin metal antenna which had lost its tip years ago.

Next, the old man pulled the cover off the battery compartment on the back of the ancient device; it was empty. He pulled the top drawer of his desk open, fished around in the back of it with his massive hands, and brought out a pack of double-A batteries.

"Yeah," he said as he installed them. "We have a

radio."

In only seconds the batteries were in. Harold set the radio up and extended the broken antenna as far as it would go. Then he began to fiddle with the knobs. The gadget crackled annoyingly, then suddenly a news station came in loud and clear.

"Stay tuned to KZIN for the latest updates on the crisis in Thornton. This is Cal Hartford, with the news.

"KZIN has just received a confirmed report that the Thornton Suburban Medical Center is currently on lockdown. Hospital administration staff tells us that mass violence has broken out in the Intensive Care Unit there following an outbreak of what is currently assumed to be a viral menace. This reporter also adds that similar reports are coming out of Monte Vista. City officials in Monte Vista have contacted the federal government for assistance with the issue, including both the Centers for Disease Control and the Federal Bureau of Investigation. Administrative staff at Suburban Medical have made reports to these branches as well, and are currently waiting on the arrival of teams for assistance with the crisis there.

Those in the Thornton and surrounding areas are advised to stay indoors under lock and key to avoid contact with any infected individuals. KZIN will continue with updates as often as they are received. Please stay tuned…"

The report was followed by some tinny brass band music that was decades outdated, and Harold turned the volume down just enough to be able to hear Kyle's thoughts. Silence came over the group.

Grunting, growling, and groaning were the most predominant sounds. Those noises were also accompanied by the shuffling of uneasy feet, the crashing of items hitting the floor, and the occasional confrontation between two of the 'monsters' outside the door.

Kyle and Diana both tried to count the beings by the sounds and where they came from, but it was impossible. So scattered and overlapped were they that it was impossible to separate them at all. The only thing that either of them was willing to bet on was the obvious fact that the 'illness' had spread to countless others in the facility, and it had managed to do so in record time.

As of yet, none of the creatures had attempted to open the door to Harold's office, but it was only a matter of time. With each unearthly grunt one or more of the others in the room would break out in a loud sob, and a couple of them had to have been heard by those on the other side of the door. Kyle had sternly signaled for silence, but the women in the office were particularly prone to losing their self-control.

The entirety of Suburban Medical Center had gone mad, or so it seemed to all of them in that room.

Megan had yawned through her tears for a couple of hours, but now she was finally asleep, though it was light and troubled. Her head rested on Diana's lap, and her small, thin body was curled up in a fetal position beneath Kyle's white coat. Every now and then her body would jerk, and Diana knew that the girl was being tormented by her own dreams.

"We have to start discussing what the heck we are going to do," Diana finally said in a voice that was just above a whisper.

All heads turned to her at once, but no one offered any suggestions right away. As a matter of fact, their looks betrayed their thoughts: that the doctor had lost her mind. But in reality, Diana knew they would not be safe in the tiny office forever.

Harold finally responded to her. "Considering the situation, I have no idea what we should do. I mean, really Doctor, do you?"

Diana shook her head. "No," she said in a resigned tone. "But I do know that with each passing minute we are only getting closer to their discovery of us. We are like fish in a barrel in here."

Kyle agreed with her. "Yes, but I don't even know if these things can be stopped, or even killed. The last time I checked on little Melanie, she had a temperature in the sixties, and she barely had any vitals at all. Personally, I think…." he glanced at Megan to make sure she wasn't awake. "I think they may already be… dead."

"I assumed as much," Diana replied. "After talking to Roy Fitch in the lab that was the only thing I could conclude. It's just unbelievable."

One of the nurses gave another sob, but now she began to cry in earnest, and fairly loudly. "I can't deal with this," she choked. "This is too crazy! I just can't handle it!"

She jumped up and headed for the door, arms up and hands in fists. Harold immediately stood, and he reached her in two long strides. Wrapping his arms around her tightly from behind he stopped her in her tracks and held her in place. For a moment her crying got louder, but Harold clasped his hand over her mouth as she kicked and struggled against him.

"I'm gonna need you to get control of yourself!" he hissed in her ear. "Dammit, you are gonna get us all killed!"

At first, she continued to fight him, but as his words sank in, the crying stopped. Harold kept a firm hold on the woman until he was sure she could be safely released, and even then he held his arms up so she could see that he would not hesitate to subdue her again. She gave him a nod of understanding as she struggled to catch her breath and head back to her seat with the others.

As if on cue, there was a bang on the other side of the office door.

Everyone in the room jumped, and all heads turned to the door. Panic filled each and every eye in the room, except for the sleeping Megan, who was oblivious to any threat. Kyle and Diana glanced at each other.

Another loud bang, followed by an extended, gurgling groan.

Diana tightened her embrace on Megan without even knowing she was doing it. "Kyle," she whispered. "What are we going to do?"

Everyone turned to Kyle, who was at a complete loss. He held his forefinger up to his lips to tell them all to be quiet, and he hoped that was all it would take to make the thing on the other side leave. But the truth was, none of them had any idea what these things were actually capable of. What if they were like dogs? What if they could smell them?

The office became more still than it had been since they got there, but the fear in the room was tangible. Even the trembling that was going on was obvious, and the hopelessness they all felt was scrawled upon their faces like so many chaotic scribbles on a blank sheet of paper. Outside the door, they heard a second voice grunting, and it eagerly joined the first.

Another bang, then another, and another. The door rattled with each strike. Harold walked to a coat tree which was positioned in a corner next to his desk. He fished around behind a coat hanging there, and after a moment he pulled out a wooden baseball bat. Without a word the man put the bat upon his shoulder, preparing himself to swing it, if necessary.

"I don't know about any of you," he whispered, "but I'm not going down without a fight."

Kyle immediately stood to offer some kind of backup to Harold, even though he was weaponless. One of the other men stood as well, and Diana gently put Megan in the corner and covered her sleeping head up with the coat before standing herself.

Another bang, but this time accompanied by a loud crack.

All of the people exchanged glances, then the two female nurses both stood and ran to the corner with the coat rack. Together they crouched and huddled there, holding each other tightly, with their eyes clenched shut. Both of their faces were dripping wet with tears.

"I've got to have something in my hands," Diana hissed, more to herself than anyone else. She was looking around the room frantically when she saw an iron up on a shelf. She raced for it and grabbed it securely in her hands and gave it a practice swing. It might have been for pressing clothes, but it was heavy enough to do damage if it had to.

Kyle took up a letter opener from Harold's desk. "I don't think it will do much, but it may deter one of them. At least I hope…"

Now it sounded like there may be several of the monsters outside the room, and the male nurse who was with them was obviously beginning to worry. He had no weapon, and he was scanning the room furiously with his eyes. They were banging on the door like mad at that point, and the noise was enough to wake little Megan up. She was sitting in the corner with her hands over her ears, and she was crying with uncontrollable sobs.

"I need something to fight with!" The male nurse began to pull drawers out of Harold's desk. "Isn't there anything else in here that I can use?"

Harold only glanced at him, his eyes shifting from the man to the door and back. "I don't know, man! Get one of the mops out of the bucket by the closet. You can take off the head and hit them with that if you have to!"

The guy quickly took the suggestion, and while he removed the mop head, the others positioned themselves in a half-circle before the door, which was now shaking consistently and had the beginnings of a crack in the middle of it. After less than a minute he joined the others. The fear in the room was thick, and not one of them was at all sure of themselves or their abilities.

"If they make it in here, just start swinging," Kyle said, his voice louder so he could be heard over the banging and yelling.

They all stood there in the office, psyching themselves up. The door continued to shake violently as each of them stabilized their footing.

Kyle opened his mouth as if to speak, just when the door was hit with such force that a section of it, right where the crack had formed, broke free and flew in toward the small, frightened group. Then, suddenly, the banging stopped, as did the loud grunting and groaning.

Everyone stopped moving. They looked at each other in silence, confusion, and fear on all of their faces.

A face appeared there in the broken gap. It was deep gray with ripped flesh and smears of blood streaked here and there. The creature was smiling, and some of his front teeth were missing. Spittle dripped down his chin.

They all stood, hearts pounding, waiting for him to come all the way in.

CHAPTER 19

The good news was that there were only three of the monsters outside Harold's office.

The bad news was that no one in the office recognized any of them. To the adults in the room, that meant that the infection had spread quickly, and none of them could conceive how many were walking around infecting others.

The situation was terribly out of control.

The nurses huddling in the corner were completely worthless. They were in such a panic that there was no talking to them. They simply cowered, cried, and screamed periodically. Megan was handling the situation far better than those grown women were.

Diana held her iron, ready for anything; Harold had his bat, Kyle his letter opener, and the male nurse stood ready with a mop handle. Sweat poured down all of their faces, and their hands trembled from the adrenaline that was coursing through their veins. The monster was wedging his body into the large, splintered gap in the door, and the other two behind him were clawing at the opening.

Harold hesitated for only a second. He rushed at the

door and swung his bat hard, connecting at first with the monster's shoulder. It screamed loudly, and its macabre smile faded fast. It then shot Harold a furious look, then began to force its way through harder and more persistently.

"Hit it again!" Megan's voice cried out. Little Megan was still in the corner, but her crying had stopped. She was now watching the adults and the monsters closely, cheering for those who were fighting for their lives. "Again!"

Harold acted on the shout and drew back the bat once more. This time when he swung the bat it hit the monster full-force in the side of the head. Its mouth and eyes flew open in what appeared to be shock. The side of its skull almost crumbled as it caved in, exposing a brain that was covered in greenish slime.

The monster collapsed in the gap, stuck there. It looked to be dead.

"The head!" Kyle shouted. "Go for their heads!"

Now the other two monsters grabbed hold of the one in the door and began to clumsily pull and tug on him, trying to get him out of their way so they could advance. Harold drew back yet again, preparing for the next one. None of them would have to wait, though. When the two monsters were able to get the first out of the door his body took a large, splintered slat of wood with it. Now the gap was more than twice its original size.

The creature closest to the door began to punch it and kick it. In its already weakened state, it gave way easily, leaving the group in the room completely open to their attack. Harold approached the second one and swung once again, but this time the monster dodged the bat, and it surprised the man. The bat flew out of his hands and hit the wall across the room.

The zombie, even in its damaged, moronic state, didn't miss a beat. It came at him quickly, with speed and what appeared to be grace. In seconds it was on the janitor, and he fell backward to the floor from the weight of the monster. It landed hard on top of him and grabbed him by the hair of his head. It buried its teeth in his cheek and easily ripped the flesh away, paying no attention to his blood-curdling screams.

Kyle rushed forward then. He straddled both Harold and the monster, and with one rapid swoop, he buried the letter opener right into the monster's temple. The thing's entire body stiffened immediately. It began to seize and twitch, then it collapsed on top of Harold, who struggled to push the thing off of him.

Meanwhile, both Diana and the male nurse were violently attacking the third monster. It was already lying on the floor just inside the office, and they were hitting it in the head with their weapons over and over. Its head resembled a broken egg, the brains and fluid spilled out in a puddle all around.

"Stop!" Kyle yelled. "We have to get out of here right now!" He glanced down at Harold, who was sitting up, calmly touching the bloody hole in his cheek. "I mean, now!"

Diana dropped the slime-covered iron to the floor

and raced over to Megan. She gathered the girl up in her arms and headed for the door. The male nurse and one female were on her heels, but the other was still sitting on the floor, her hands over her ears, screaming at the top of her lungs.

"We have to go!"

Harold opened his eyes and turned his head to the screaming female in the corner. A smile started to come over his face. That was all it took for Kyle to pick up and bolt from the room full-force.

He noticed that Diana was headed for the stairs. "No, Diana! The elevator! They are going to be using the stairs!"

The group ran for the elevator and pushed the 'UP' button. While they waited for it to come from the second floor, Kyle ran back and looked through the door to see Harold sitting on top of the nurse. He was chewing, his face covered in blood, and making terrible crunching sounds. He ran back.

"The change is too fast," Kyle said just as the elevator door opened.

Two people were inside, one a nurse and the other a man in a suit. She was crying, and he was trying to comfort her, but both appeared normal. The group crowded onto the elevator, and Kyle began to frantically push the button for the sixth floor over and over.

When the door closed, he turned to the two newcomers. "Are you both okay?"

"Yes," the man replied while the woman sobbed. "What the heck?"

"It's a long story," Kyle said. He turned to Diana. "We are going to six, where the main conference room is. It is solid, with heavy oak doors, no windows. We should be safe there, and there is a television as well."

All of them watched the numbers as the elevator rose, concern about stopping cemented in their minds. At six Kyle said, "Okay, the conference room is to the right, first set of double doors. Make a beeline for it, and don't stop for anything. We don't know who is going to be there."

The doors opened to complete silence. Kyle pressed the button to keep the doors open and poked his head out: there was nothing and no one to be seen.

"Okay, on three," he said. "One… two… three!"

All of them took off like a shot. One of the conference room doors was slightly open, and Kyle grabbed it and held it open so the others could get in easily. Then he flipped the light switch and closed and locked the door.

"Help me move a couple of these tables in front of the doors, will you?" he asked the man in the suit. "It would be best to reinforce it as much as possible."

Diana noticed a large window at one end of the room. "I thought you said there were no windows!"

"None that are accessible from inside the building, obviously," he replied. "That one gives us a view of the outside, and we are on the sixth floor, Diana. We're safe."

While the men moved the tables, Diana put little Megan in a large, leather chair by the window. She then walked over to the big window and opened the blinds a bit. Down below it looked so peaceful. There was nothing in the parking lot but cars. Not people, not monsters. At the head of the main drive, she could see orange cones and flashing red and blue lights: the police. There were also fire trucks and a few people within view, but not many.

"I don't see any of the monsters down there," she said.

Kyle put down his end of the second table, positioning it firmly against the first. He then wiped the sweat off his forehead and replied, "Well, we are on lockdown. They probably have the issue contained in the hospital. It is a relief to know that, anyway."

She nodded. "I'm going to turn on the television. We need to know what's going on for sure; no guessing."

"I agree," the man in the suit said.

They all found chairs to sit in while Diana got the television going. It immediately came on to a special news broadcast. She turned it up, so they could hear, but not loud enough to attract any attention from outside the conference room.

"According to local police, the situation is indeed dire." A blond woman with a slight smile was relaying the situation at Suburban Medical in Thornton. "The hospital has been on lockdown for several hours now, and no civilians or officers have gone inside as of yet. Suburban Medical is surrounded with armed police while city officials discuss how the problem is going to be dealt with. Also, with the release of the news that the Aspen Lumiosa pen is to blame for the outbreak, the entire town of Monte Vista has been shut down and all outlets in and out of it have been blocked off. Here's Sam Donovan, on location at Suburban Medical Center. Sam?"

"Thanks, Emily." The picture changed to a male anchor who was obviously outside the hospital. In the background were countless police and other emergency vehicles. "As you can see, the Suburban Medical Center here in Thornton is under lock and key, and authorities and medical assistance are surrounding the entire medical campus. The outbreak, according to the CDC, has been caused by an infectious ink which was released a short time ago by Aspen Stationers' Supply in Monte Vista. The entire town of Monte Vista is on quarantine, but only Suburban Medical Center is shut down in this area.

"There is no need for anyone to panic, according to authorities. The pens have all been taken off the shelves, so as long as you do not destroy any pens, you will reduce the risk of exposure to you or your children, and therefore you should be safe. If you have one of these pens, please call the number on the screen for collection procedures. Infection becomes apparent almost immediately, according to the CDC, so if you or your friends or loved ones have shown no sign of infection, you are safe. They are working to not only create an antidote but also to clean up the problem in all infected areas of the state. Reports have also been made in

Kansas, New Mexico, Utah, and Wyoming. If you come into contact with an infected person, attacking the head is the only way to stop them.

"Stay with Fox 31 for all the latest updates of the Lumiosa crisis. Back to you, Emily."

Diana turned the volume down and looked at the others. "Well, at least they figured out what caused this, and they are working to find a solution. I just wish we could get out of here."

"That's going to take some time, obviously," Kyle replied. "They have to figure out how to get the infected ones under control, or they run the risk of them getting out in public."

The man in the tie spoke up. "It seems pretty futile to me. How the heck are they going to get rid of all of them, and be sure that they have?"

Everyone was silent for a minute, then Megan spoke up in a soft voice. "I say we keep watching the news. It's not for us to worry about right now."

Diana turned to the girl and smiled. She ruffled her hair with her fingers and said, "Come here little one. I think you might be the only sane person here, don't you agree?"

Megan only smiled and snuggled against Diana. The girl was right: they all needed to worry about staying safe, and let the hard work be done by the police. After all, that was what they were for.

Hopefully, they would figure things out before it was too late.

CHAPTER 20

Monte Vista, now labeled as Ground Zero, was undergoing a 'clean sweep.'

After extensive meetings, which rendered no real solutions, there was really only one conclusion to come to. It was disappointing, to say the least, but even Mayor Donnelly had to agree. His entire town had gone into hiding, and no one was safe. Sure, they knew the cause of the issue, but no one could seem to figure out how to reverse it. Just standing at the window in his office was enough to send jolts of panic through his body and the bodies of everyone who had a halfway decent view.

The infected had to be destroyed; it was as simple as that. But how? How could it be done?

What if someone was out wandering the street who wasn't infected; wouldn't they be harmed in the efforts? Well, according to Mel Potter of the Department of Defense, no one had any time to worry about that. All of the citizens of Monte Vista had been warned, more than once, as a matter of fact, to stay inside under lock and key. Even the high school had been offered for safety. If someone were out 'wandering around' it would be their own fault if they were caught up in the solution, whatever it was.

Mayor Donnelly and his assistant, along with Cole and Clemons, were in the mayor's office having a conference call with the President himself and all of his advisors. Together they were brainstorming for the best possible solution, one that would allow them to wipe out the infected while simultaneously causing as little harm to the healthy public as possible.

So far, they had nothing.

"Do you have an estimate of how many people may be wandering the streets there in Monte Vista, Donnelly?" The president's tone was one of both frustration and confusion.

Donnelly took a deep breath. "No, I really don't. I would like to believe that there are none, and that all of the civilians have followed the directives we have issued, but who's to say?" Just then gunfire rang out in the street out front of city hall, audible enough to be heard on the conference phone.

"Well, sir," interjected General Monroe, "We can hardly move forward with any kind of plan of action if you have no idea what the heck is going on in your town!"

Master Sergeant Michael Abano finally spoke as well. "I agree. Even though we have no concrete plan, we really can't even put one together without knowledge of the current town status."

After listening for a moment, Charles Cole got the feeling that a full-fledged argument was on the horizon. "Listen, listen. Men, with all due respect, I don't see how you can expect the mayor to know much of anything. The truth is, he has been locked down just like everyone else. Let's go with what we know."

"What do we know, Cole?" President Baker asked.

Cole cleared his throat. "We know that the 'Deadwalkers' are seeking human flesh. We know that the town has been on lockdown for some time. We know that there is, as of yet, no antidote for the infection. And we know that the only way they can be stopped is by destroying the head."

"So, what do you propose?" This question came from presidential advisor Steven Holt. "You realize that any solution we come up with here will likely be implemented in the other locations. Monte Vista is in deeper than any other place, and we even have an entire hospital on lockdown in Thornton. We need to come up with something, and fast."

Mel Potter spoke. "Any solution runs the risk of civilian casualties, men. Simply enough, its War, and we all know it." The Secretary of Defense paused. "It has been proven time after time, battle after battle, and this one is no exception."

The men were all quiet for an uncomfortable amount of time. General Monroe finally spoke, and when he did, his tone was very firm. "With Monte Vista being in the worst condition, with the 'Deadwalkers,' running the streets, we need to take action that is direct and forceful. I have an idea, but none of you will like it much. Personally, I don't see any other option."

"Well," President Baker said after Monroe paused.

"Out with it, man!"

"Okay," he continued. "This is what I think: they are wandering around, they are fighting with each other, and they are searching for any living human they can find to attack and eat, correct?"

"Correct," the mayor replied.

"I say our infantrymen suit up. I say we send them out, up and down every single street, and I say they plant a bullet in the head of everyone they encounter showing symptoms. Shoot first and ask questions later," Monroe concluded.

Now all the men went into thought mode. True, the mayor considered, they had come up with no alternatives. They could not continue to simply hide out and hope for the best; they needed to eliminate the threat, and they needed to do it fast. It wasn't as if they could bomb the area, or set it on fire. No, Monroe's solution seemed to be the most reasonable and acceptable out of all the considerations, which had been few.

"I like it," Mayor Donnelly said.

President Baker asked, "What about concern for the public?"

"Well, as you mentioned, everyone has been told to lock down," he replied. "What other realistic options do we have? No one can seem to think of anything safer or better."

Baker was silent for a long moment, and no one interrupted his train of thought. Finally, he said, "Fine. Monroe and Abano, I want you to confer with the others and work out a plan of action. Both branches need to put armed troops together and have as many as you need to be flown into the affected cities. I want the entire plan ready to go by sunrise tomorrow, understood?"

"Yes sir," rang throughout the room.

"Fine. Report back to me by twenty-three hundred hours," Baker concluded. "I want to hear that everything is a go the next time we speak."

With that, the president abruptly ended his side of the call.

Chief Master Sergeant Abano spoke up. "We will confer by telephone and formulate a plan of action for the troops. We will call when we call the president tonight, so remain by the phone, understood?"

"Absolutely," Donnelly said. The call was completely disconnected.

"Get the latest maps out. We don't have any time to lose."

All at once the men took action, and the planning of 'Deadwalker Clean-up' began.

∞

Captain Hertz's press conference had gone very well; he had managed to professionally stress the importance of the public to remain safe at home, while answering the press' questions without sparking panic. Surprisingly the streets cleared up quickly.

Hertz sent officers around the city, armed with high-powered rifles, to see if they could identify any of the murderous 'people.'

Randy had spoken with the FBI, and then the CDC. He gave them all the information he could, though he didn't think that any of it would truly help their purpose: the complete eradication of the monsters which the Lumiosa ink had produced. They did make him aware of one thing they had learned: the creatures could be destroyed only by destroying their heads. Otherwise, complete and total evasion would have to be the tactic until the government came up with a solid plan of eradication.

Now, Captain Hertz sat in his office with Randy. The two of them had steaming cups of coffee in front of them, and they were casually discussing the situation there in Monte Vista. It seemed as if the town was in pretty good shape.

"Well, with few monsters being found here, I feel like we are a step ahead," the captain said.

Randy blew on his coffee and took a quick sip. "The fact of the matter, Captain, is that you put Aspen on lockdown right away. That quarantine was probably far more powerful than any of us understand. Clemons from the CDC told me that they would be visiting the factory and destroying all the rats in the lab. Heck, they may even be there now, for all we know."

Hertz nodded and sat back in his chair. He felt like much of the weight he had been bearing emotionally for the last few days was finally easing up. He closed his eyes and took a deep breath; he felt nothing but relief.

Right then his phone rang.

"This is Captain Hertz," he answered.

Randy sat back himself and focused on his coffee. The last thing on his mind was the phone call, though he could hear the voice on the other end, gabbing and enunciating. He gave the captain a glance; he seemed to be calm, so it was likely okay.

"That's wonderful," Hertz said into the receiver. "I have already sent several of my men out, armed, in squad cars, to patrol and search for any of them that may have slipped through our fingers. They have reported a small amount to me thus far."

The voice continued to gab, then Hertz said, "That would be fine. As a matter of fact, a second pair of eyes never hurt anyone. If your men stop by here, we can confer and determine how they want to do things in cooperation with my men... agreed?"

When Hertz hung up the phone, Randy was looking at him expectantly. "Good news?" he asked.

"That was the FBI," he replied. "They wanted to let me know they had to totally destroy the lab at Aspen; and most of the rest of the factory. Personally, I couldn't care less at this point."

Randy smiled and nodded, then the captain continued. "They are also going to send a few Army troops through town to assist in tracking down any stragglers. Those troops will be here within a few hours. I'm just going to advise that they use GPS to scour the town, and use force as desired."

"What if you suffer losses?" Randy asked. "I know my family is safe, but we live out of town a tad. But what about the others here? What if someone is actually outside, in the wrong place at the wrong time?"

Hertz sat forward, a serious look on his face. "We had a press conference; we released the news on the radio and TV. All I can say is that the citizens should be indoors until otherwise instructed. I cannot worry about that now, not when we have to ensure their safety by patrolling, not to mention shooting to kill."

It was easy enough to accept. Randy and Hertz left the office and made their way to the staff break room to get a bite to eat. Hertz told his secretary to call him when the military arrived.

It seemed that things might finally wrap up for the best in Monte Vista.

CHAPTER 21

Shortly after Kyle, Diana, and the rest of the group settled into the conference room and watched the news, Diana picked up the telephone and dialed 911. She made the operator aware of their presence on the sixth floor of Suburban Medical and asked how things were moving along as far as getting the infected under control. She and the others wanted nothing more than to be out of that building and at home with the people they loved.

It wasn't to be, at least, not right at that moment. The operator patched her through to an officer who was down on the street. He listened to her explanation of who she was, who was with her, where they were, and why they were there. He tried to comfort her and reassure her that if they all just stayed put they would eventually be out, but he couldn't give her any type of time frame. He simply told her, repetitively, to stay put and sit tight.

They were all exhausted. They managed to get some much-needed sleep, only for a very brief period of time. They also only slept in what seemed to be shifts, though none of it had rhyme or reason. All but Megan were rested and awake, four hours had passed since they first arrived at the conference room. Now they were simply ravenous. They all managed to ignore the hunger pangs, which worked fairly well until Megan woke up.

"How are you doing, little lady?" Kyle asked the tired-eyed child.

She shrugged shyly and offered a small grin. "I don't know."

Diana tousled her hair once again; the action had become something of a habit during their time together. "Do you feel better since you got some sleep, dear?"

"I guess so," she replied. "I'm really, really hungry."

Diana immediately looked up at Kyle, and he glanced at the others briefly. "Well, I am pretty familiar with this floor. I mean, we have tons of administration meetings up here. There is a kitchen and staff room across the main area. I could go and see if there is anything in there that would provide us with sustenance."

"I'll go with you," Suit-and-Tie Man said to him. "Better to do things in twos, I think. What could we carry with us? I mean, for safety's sake."

Kyle looked around and began to take in all the objects in the room with his eyes. Besides the tables and chairs there was a smaller table against one wall; on it was a coffee pot, Styrofoam cups, a basket with powdered creamers and sugars, and another with coffee stirrers.

Next to the door was a coat rack made of metal. It had hangers on it, but they were attached; the users had to hang their coat while the hanger remained on the rod. He saw nothing that resembled personal protection in any way.

After a moment Kyle said, "Okay, it looks like slim pickings in here. I say the two of us head out; Diana, you lock the door behind us. We will run for the kitchen area and take a look around. If we see anything or anyone who poses a threat, well, we grab the thing closest to us, whatever that may be. Agreed?"

"Agreed."

Both of the men stood and stretched their limbs before heading to the doors. Diana was right behind them, ready to lock the doors once they were out. She watched in silence as they moved the tables carefully, trying to not make any noise. Once that was finished, Kyle held his finger up to his lips, unlocked the main door, turned the knob, and poked his head out.

Just as when they first arrived on the sixth floor, the place was empty, almost what you would call 'dead.' The lights were on overhead, but all of the desks just sat there. Most of them looked as if they had been suddenly deserted. Chairs pushed away, computers still lit up, and papers with pens on top of them still sitting, waiting for their owners to return. Obviously, everyone had made a run for it at the drop of a hat.

He turned back to the group and gave a single nod before looking at Tie Man. "Are you ready to go for it?"

The man nodded back at him, positioning himself to bolt from the room.

"Make sure you follow me; I know where we are

going, okay?"

The man nodded again.

"Okay," Kyle said. "Let's go!"

The men ran full-force from the conference room, and Diana rushed to the door and closed it and locked it.

They ran to the kitchen, weaving between desks and chairs as they headed for their goal. On the way there they saw absolutely nothing to worry them or make them afraid. When Kyle opened the kitchen he was relieved to see that it was empty, and he carefully shut the door behind them, holding his finger to his lips once again.

"Did you see or hear anything?" he asked in a whisper.

Tie Man shook his head. "Nothing."

With that, the two of them made their way to the cupboards and refrigerators. While Tie Man went quietly through each cupboard, Kyle opened the refrigerator. He was happy to see numerous bagged lunches and even a couple of thermal lunch containers. He grabbed an armful of them, several cans of soda, and a small container of milk.

"How's this?" he asked his companion.

The man smiled at him. "Perfect." He then held up a handful of plastic forks and spoons. "Just in case."

"Great. Let's go."

They left the kitchen quickly, and not at all as quietly as they had arrived. In their relief to have found so much food, they seemed to have forgotten the danger of their situation. They were even meandering back to the conference room, their need to run all but forgotten. It was then that they heard the noise.

Kyle turned suddenly toward the sound, which was much like the breaking of a pencil. There, approximately twenty feet away from the two men, standing right next to the entrance to the fire stairs, was one of the monsters. It appeared to smile and lick its lips in anticipation.

"Hey…" Kyle began, speaking to Tie Man. He wanted to tell him to run, to get to the conference room as soon as possible, but the words would not come from his lips as he wanted them to.

But Tie Man heard him. "What? What are you…?" He turned around, and he, too, saw the monster. It was now beginning to limp, slowly but surely, toward them.

"R… R… Run!" The word came out of Kyle's mouth in nothing more than a hoarse whisper. He began to back up, his eyes still glued to the inhuman-looking creature that was making its way toward them both.

"Run, now!"

Kyle suddenly turned, his hands and arms clinging blindly to the bags and cans in his arms. He passed Tie Man, then glanced over his shoulder as he ran, just in time to realize that his companion was literally frozen to his spot.

Kyle reached the conference room door and, keeping his eyes on both Tie Man and the monster, began to kick at it with all his might. "Open up! Let us in! Let us in now!"

He could hear Diana fiddling with the lock on the other side, but it didn't matter. In only seconds the monster closed the gap between itself and Tie Man, who, at the last second, seemed to be able to try to get away. Unfortunately, it was just too late.

Tie man turned and tried to bolt toward Kyle, but his right foot caught his left, and he stumbled. He hit the floor hard, and plastic utensils flew through the air in all directions. The monster reached him and dropped to his knees next to the scrambling man. Then the monster grabbed him by his hair and began to forcefully pound the man's forehead into the hard floor, over and over again. After several hits, blood began to pour from the man's head.

The conference room door flew open, and Kyle went in quickly. He dropped the bags and cans to the floor, then turned around to relock the door just in time to see the monster scooping a handful of the twitching man's brains into his mouth. He closed and locked the door quickly, gagging hard the entire time.

After a moment he gained control of himself. "Help me. Help me move the tables, all of them!"

The male nurse ran forward, contributing for the first time since they had arrived upstairs. Together, he and Kyle began moving the heavy tables and placing them on their sides up against the door. They moved all of them, this time. He wanted as much weight against the door as possible. Tie Man would be turning soon, and then there would be two of them trying to get into the conference room for... fresh meat.

When the tables were all moved Kyle turned around and sat down hard on the floor on his bottom. He put his head into his hands and, for the first time since the whole thing began, he was afraid. He was silent, his breath the only audible noise coming from his body.

When he looked up the first thing he saw was Megan. She was clinging to Diana with a look on her face that gave away the level of fear she was experiencing. Kyle offered the girl a smile.

"I'm fine, honey," he said to her. "I'm really fine."

There was a bang at the door.

"Ignore it," Kyle continued as he stood up. He grabbed a few bags of food and headed toward the others. "There is no way they are going to get in here; at least, not right away. If we stay quiet, they are bound to wander off."

"Kyle," Diana whispered. "Are you sure?"

He nodded at her, the smile still plastered to his face. "As sure as I will ever be about anything."

All of them sat down on the floor in a circle and began to unpack their food. The entire time the banging on the door continued; they could even hear the frustrated grunting and screaming coming from the monsters outside. They all focused on ignoring them, but the noise made it terribly hard for any of them to eat.

∞

Down at the parking lot entrance of Suburban Medical, Thornton Police Chief Dan Davis was speaking on his cellular phone to one Charles Cole of the FBI.

Cole was telling him that they were going to be setting forth a plan to go through the town of Monte Vista and shoot every living thing in sight. Cole was telling him it was the only way they could see to rid the town of the infected people that were running amok, murdering the citizens. Cole was also letting him know that, if the plan worked, at sunrise Suburban Medical would be next on the list.

"Have any of the Deadwalkers managed to escape the facility?" Cole asked Davis.

Davis knit his brow. "Deadwalkers? Oh, you must mean the monsters. No, sir. One attempted, but we put him down and secured the compromised area. The hospital is now completely secure, though we don't know how many normal people are trying to survive inside."

"And you won't until this is over," Cole finished for him. "Now, we will be contacting you in the morning to let you know how all of us are going to proceed to help all of you in Thornton to solve your problem. Keep your phone charged, Chief. It's going to be a very long night."

CHAPTER 22

Helicopters flew the skies over Monte Vista, having no regard for the early morning hours. After all, loss of sleep was a very small price to pay for the inhabitants of a town threatened by countless zombies. And to be honest, no one cared.

"Okay, men!" General Abel Monroe was pacing back and forth in front of a massive number of troops, delivering a message that needed to be heard loud and clear. He spoke through a large bullhorn, and he used the loudest voice possible. "Today is the day! Now is the time! We are going to rid Monte Vista of the Deadwalkers!"

The troops stood silent, in rapt attention. This was only the Army whom he was addressing in the chain-link confined area provided for that purpose at the local high school football field.

"You are each assigned to an outlet road," Monroe continued. "As you know, you will line up, according to assigned platoons, across the road which you have been assigned to. You will begin to walk into town. All of you have a listing, which is in possession of your platoon leaders, as to all of the roads you must cover. You will shoot on sight whoever you see or encounter that appears infected or abnormal. It must be a headshot; you must shoot to kill!"

Monroe paused for effect. "From here you will be transported via utility vehicle to your assigned road. Be ready, and be on a careful lookout at all times. There is absolutely no room for compassion or mercy; these things are the enemy. Look at them any way you must to get the job done. They are the enemy, and this, boys, is a war!"

"Sir, yes, sir!"

"Do I have the understanding of all of you?" he asked in a mean voice.

"Sir, yes, sir!"

"Do any of you want to pussy out? Now is the time to do it, girls!"

"Sir, no, sir!"

Monroe smiled and nodded at them all. "Good! That is exactly what I want to hear. I want you to go out and make mincemeat out of these beasts. I want to be able to load their mangled corpses on a truck and haul them out of Monte Vista so these families can get back to their lives. Understood?"

"Sir, yes, sir!"

"Now, sunrise is just under seven minutes," he continued. "We will wait here for a call from the Air Force that their men are ready. Stand at attention, men!"

He heard a snicker float through the group, and he had to fight back a smile. They were laughing about the Air Force being included in the mission. "No laughter here, ladies! We are all on the same side, am I understood?"

Silence, then the obligatory "Sir, yes, sir!"

∞

The Air Force's Chief Master Sergeant Michael Abano was addressing his men in the school gymnasium. Abano's men went through a nearly identical briefing, including laughter when the Army was mentioned. It seemed attitudes were the same all over. All of the men were nervous, and even a few of them were downright scared. After all, they were dealing with something that they had heard about only from books or science fiction movies.

When his speech was over, Abano flipped open his cell and called Monroe, whom he had programmed into speed dial. "We're ready," he stated simply.

Within minutes he had his men marching out of the gymnasium and through the secured back door of the high school, which led to the football field. The field itself was surrounded by guards and large trucks, which would haul the men to their assigned destinations. By five thirty, the trucks were running and loaded with armed men.

Abano and Monroe sat in the leading vehicle, waiting for word that the last of the men were on board and ready to go. Monroe received text, and he looked over at Abano. He gave the man a bloodthirsty smile.

"Are we ready, Chief Master Sergeant?"

The man grinned back. "We are absolutely ready,

General. Let's go get their blood!"

The chain-link gate before them was opened by two armed footmen, who pulled them wide for the trucks to pass through. One by one they were driven out of the area and turned their individual directions. It wouldn't be long now; not long at all.

According to calculations, the entire town of Monte Vista would be swept clean in a few hours.

CHAPTER 23

For all intents and purposes, Captain Hertz was told that the town of Monte Vista, Colorado, appeared to be in the clear.

Not only had Aspen Stationers' Supply Company been completely burned to the ground, but the land and remaining bits of the building were sprayed with a rat extermination solution. There were no human bodies anywhere on the grounds. The quarantine was continued, but only because of the chemicals sprayed. It was fenced off, and security was placed around it with guns and gas masks.

Troops came into the small area, sent on orders from the head of the Department of Defense, Mel Potter. Since the town was thought to be free of threat, it was over in less than an hour. Just as suspected, no threat was found, whatsoever.

Hertz held another press conference, this time to alert the town to the newfound sense of freedom they were all entitled to. He wanted them all to know, as soon as possible, that the issue was over. Not only was the town free of the monsters, but Aspen was no longer in operation, and it never would be again. The only repercussions for the company would be for board members and shareholders who had scurried around so energetically to cover up Dr. Carstens' findings regarding the Lumiosa ink. Yes, Captain Hertz assured everyone, criminal charges would be sought.

Monte Vista, Colorado, the place where it all began, labeled Ground Zero, was finally free, and it seemed it had suffered far less than anyone else.

∞

At 7:05 in the morning, Thornton Police chief Dan Davis, who was on easily his thirtieth cup of coffee, answered his cell phone from the Suburban Medical Center parking entrance. He had been waiting all night for that ring, and when it finally came to his relief was obvious to every single person around him.

"Agent Cole. What's the verdict?"

"We have been in action here in Monte Vista for about an hour and fifteen minutes, and I have to tell you that it seems this was the right route to take with these… things," Cole replied. "I want you to know that President Baker is ordering that a couple of groups be sent to Suburban Medical Center to eliminate the problem there, but before he does, I have a few questions I need to ask you for the safety of those involved."

"Shoot," Davis said.

Davis could hear Cole shuffling through some papers. "Okay," he finally said, "how many men do you have in attendance, and where are you located?"

"Well, at the current time the count is just under

eighty-three men, and we are stationed all around the hospital, as well as at the entrance. My men have the campus completely secured."

There was a pause, which Davis assumed was so that Cole could jot down notes.

Cole continued. "Do you have any idea if any civilians are in the building at the current time?"

"Yes, sir. We have word from several individuals; however, the only ones who have managed to keep in consistent contact is a group who says they are located in the sixth-floor administration conference room," he said.

"How do you know that? How often have they called?"

Davis rolled his eyes. "The last call was approximately twenty minutes ago when they asked if help was on the way. There are five of them, I think, and they have a twelve-year-old girl with them. Two doctors, two nurses, and a girl."

"Okay," Cole said, then he took a deep breath. "We will need to find a way to get them out of there before we advance. Does the conference room have a window of any kind? Is there a way to access them from outside, if at all possible?"

Now Davis began to stroll toward the hospital and look the building over, though he had no idea what he was looking at or looking for. "I don't know, sir, but I can certainly find out."

"Do that," Cole said. "Troops are going to be there within the hour, and we will need answers. Find out the same things from any other people in the building who happen to contact you. We need to save civilians if at all possible."

"Yes, sir." Davis hung up the phone and turned to one of the deputy sheriffs. "I need to find out if the sixth-floor conference room has a window; we need to get those people out if at all possible. Get on it!"

As his man ran off, Davis continued to stare at the building. If there were others in there, and they were still alive, why had they not called him back? Well, in the long run, it didn't matter. Soon the troops would be there, and they would save who they could, but they would take out anyone who got in their way.

Davis couldn't worry about that.

CHAPTER 24

It took only three hours for all of the troops, both Army and Air Force, to completely clear the streets of Monte Vista, Colorado, of the Deadwalkers.

No one came out of the homes. No one walked on the gravel roads on the outskirts of town. No one even tried to threaten the mission that the United States government was in the middle of. So frightened, so petrified was the public that they simply stayed inside their homes and let it all happen.

One by one, bullet by bullet, brain by brain, the Deadwalkers were eliminated from the face of the Earth.

They were loaded onto trucks and transported to the workstations which were set up by the CDC, where they would be studied and scrutinized. Down at city hall in Monte Vista, they received reports on each and every single one, and charges were pressed on those who were criminally negligent from Aspen. Next of kin were contacted, and the circle continued to move, slowly but surely.

At exactly 10:28 the mission was completed. There were no more Deadwalkers; it was as easy as that. All that remained were grief-stricken families and terrified children. Mayor Tom Donnelly addressed the public to inform everyone that, while they would likely want to remain in their homes while the mess was cleaned up, the horror story that had filled the last few days was finally over. He said it with a smile and a confidence that enabled everyone watching to breathe huge sighs of relief.

Helicopters were sent, along with limited troops, to Thornton, to the Suburban Medical Center. It was time to clean up the last of it in Colorado. Troops were also in the other states, and they were dealing with the issue in those places just as expeditiously. The outbreaks in the other states were not nearly as bad, and the biggest concern left was Suburban Medical Center and the people holed up in the sixth-floor conference room…

∞

The same morning, three helicopters flew into the airspace over Suburban Medical Center. At the same time, five military trucks, filled with troops, arrived as well. They pulled into the entrance, and the officer in command found Dan Davis easily enough.

"Chief Davis, I'm Lieutenant Faust of the United States Army," he began. Have you found out whether or not we can access the area with the civilians?"

Davis immediately snapped to attention. "Absolutely, sir. It is the strip of three windows on the south side of the building, six levels up. I have been in telephone contact, and one Dr. Diana Moss will be waiting at the window for your instructions."

"Fine," Faust said. "Now, I will need all men to clear the entrance to the lot and the lot itself. Once we retrieve the innocent, we will literally barnstorm this building. You have no other civilians that you are aware of?"

Davis shook his head, a look of deep regret on his face. "No, sir. None."

After a curt nod, Faust ran to the lot. A helicopter had landed in the far end of it. Davis ordered all cars out of the vicinity, then watched as Faust boarded the chopper and it lifted off the ground.

Finally, this would all come to an end.

The chopper took flight, and for the next half-hour, everyone on the ground watched as the men inside of it communicated with the people on the sixth floor through the window. They watched in horror as the people were brought from the building into the craft. It was terrifying, but it was necessary, and when the very last person was transferred those on the ground broke out in deafening cheers.

They were all one step closer to the goal.

Television cameras and reporters were set up on the ground, capturing every last thing they possibly could. Many tears were shed when the people were saved, but the stress resumed when the troops entered the actual facility. From ten minutes until eleven all the way to twelve thirty, shots rang out from inside the hospital. At twelve forty-three the Army commander gave the 'all clear,' and trucks pulled up to eliminate the bodies of the monsters from the building.

It happened that fast. The horrible nightmare which had suffocated Colorado and other states was suddenly over. People were freed and safe, and the monsters were all dead. Interviews were held, and charges were pressed.

Life, as everyone knew it, began to go back to normal.

EPILOGUE

Monte Vista, 2 weeks later…

Things began to get back to normal for everyone; Captain Hertz was a local hero. He was heralded for acting so quickly at the Aspen plant and quarantining the facility the way he did. If not for him, who knew what would have happened in that tiny little town?

Randy returned home to his wife and family. He narrowly dodged legal charges himself. If not for the fact that he walked away from the bigwigs at Aspen, he would be facing a jail sentence. Instead, he was hired by a makeup company who wanted a scientist with integrity. In Monte Vista, many had to virtually start their lives over. Out of all the places affected, Monte Vista suffered the greatest loss. Many locals relocated. Some died when the troops tore through. No one there would ever be the same, and Mayor Donnelly knew that all too well. He discovered that his own son had been infected and killed by the troops, and he committed suicide shortly after the incident.

In Thornton at the Suburban Medical Center, the only people to come out alive were the small group in the conference room. Kyle, Diana, Megan, and the others were spared. Diana took custody of one very disturbed Megan and began adoption proceedings almost right away. Everyone else in the facility was killed, either by the Deadwalkers or the military.

At the former home of Linda and little Timmy Abbott, there was no life at all.

Her small house, only two city blocks from the Aspen Company, sat empty and dark. Timmy's little toys were still on the sidewalk, and no one had been there since the outbreak. Not even Linda's family could bear to set foot on the desolate, lonely property.

Now, two weeks later, out in the country, the house still sat in silence.

A blue sedan blew a tire right in front of the place on an empty dirt road. Miles Flatt, a traveling businessman, pulled his car over in the darkness to change the tire. He had promised his wife he would be home tonight, and he didn't have time to spare.

He propped his flashlight up and whistled while he loosened the lug nuts.

Forty feet away, the ground started to move.

A squeaking came from the spot as the dirt was being disturbed, and after a moment a small, furry creature covered in dried blood and grime emerged. What was left of its nose twitched, and it turned toward the sound of the whistling.

ENTREATY

This book was made possible by reviews from readers like you. Reviews fuel my creativity. If you enjoyed this novel, I implore you to please write a review and share your experience on the retailer's website. The livelihood for authors is entirely dependent on reviews, and I must say, it is the largest obstacle as a struggling author that I have encountered. Please tell a friend, tell a loved one about this read. With your help, I will be one step closer to overcoming this obstacle. In return, I thank you from the bottom of my heart, and sincerely appreciate your time and effort.

Humbled, with gratitude,
R.W.K. Clark

ABOUT THE AUTHOR

I am a father of two beautiful children, Jon and Kim. They are my motivating forces; they are the lighthouse in this vast ocean. In my life, they are the air that I breathe; they are the oasis in this desert of uncertainty. They are my greatest joy in life and my number one priority. I have a long list of hobbies, and I attribute that to my lust for life! I like to surround myself with positive people, who share the same interests. Family values, the arts, outdoors, nature, and travel are tops on my list. I embrace attending cultural and artistic events because I believe dramatic self-expression is the window to the soul. I wear my heart on my sleeve, and I still believe in chivalry, and I always treat people the way I want to be treated.

www.rwkclark.com

www.ingramcontent.com/pod-product-compliance
Lightning Source LLC
Chambersburg PA
CBHW030304180626
46810CB00003B/916